My Name is
Sei Shōnagon

My Name is
Sei Shōnagon

Jan Blensdorf

THE OVERLOOK PRESS
WOODSTOCK & NEW YORK

First published in the United States in 2003 by
The Overlook Press, Peter Mayer Publishers, Inc.
Woodstock & New York

WOODSTOCK:
One Overlook Drive
Woodstock, NY 12498
www.overlookpress.com
[for individual orders, bulk and special sales, contact our Woodstock office]

NEW YORK:
141 Wooster Street
New York, NY 10012

∞ The paper used in this book meets the requirements for paper
permanence as described in the ANSI Z39.48-1992 standard.

Library of Congress Cataloging-in-Publication Data

Blensdorf, Jan.
My name is Sei Shōnagon / Jan Blensdorf.
p. cm.
2. Hospital patients—Fiction. 2. Young women—Fiction.
3. Tokyo (Japan)—Fiction. I. Title.
PR9619.4.B57M9 2003   823'.92—dc21   2003054930

Printed in the United States of America
ISBN 1-58567-443-5
1 3 5 7 9 8 6 4 2

My Name is
Sei Shōnagon

TODAY, RAIN is the first thing I know. I smell it and hear it at the same time. And my heart beating deep rapid beats into the pillow with the quickness of the waking.

Before they come to turn and reposition me, there is a closer scent of heavy hospital linen, and an image forming in my mind: the *kanji* for rain, which it is said began as a drawing of drops falling from a cloud, the picture to which we have given the sound '*ame*'. The English word for rain is a woman alone, looking out of a window into the rain as into herself, watching it join the sea until they blend without horizon. And then I drift beyond rain, to the French '*âme*', which has no picture but is simply a beautiful colour without boundaries – the word for soul.

I don't even know if you are still alive. I'm going to talk to you anyway. I'm going to tell you everything I can remember.

There is an incense shop in a small street leading off Omotosando. It is called *The Bridge of Dreams*. And upstairs, where the scent from below lingers as softly as the memory of a lover's hand or tongue, there is a room. While the stairs leading to it are narrow, the space that opens out before you is large, empty apart from a painted screen, the floor covered in fine-woven *tatami*. Behind the doors of the cupboards at one end lie all kinds of things, hidden things. But the room itself is completely open to view, an untroubled surface, like calm water.

The shop below is as restful as a temple compared to the street outside. On the counter, on any given day, a small burner sits in readiness to release the perfumed essence of aloeswood or *jinkoh*. In the sixth century a great log of this wood drifted ashore, on to the island of Awaji, near Kobe. The scent that filled the air when the timber began to burn was so incredible that the islanders decided to present it to the Empress. They had made an extraordinary find – a source of one of the rarest fragrances then known, which had come to Japan with Buddhism less than fifty years before. As always, a sliver of the same species will be lying with others on the counter in the little shop off Omotosando, its tendrils of smoke still coiled in wait like a promise, ready to thread their way out into the polluted air of Tokyo – the pulse of another age.

Soon the hollow metal bird above the door will move with its child's toy sound between a ring and a rattle, and someone will enter. The client will take time to look, to muse, will consider the merits of one choice over another, and will then wait for the chip to be placed on the burner, for the warmth to coax it to life.

To breathe it in, eyes half-closed, is to be entered by another world – of revelations, infinitely subtle. This is what the Chinese were the first to call *Wenxiang* – listening to incense.

When the air is heavy with rain I can hear the occasional high-pitched scream of metal on metal. We must be somewhere near a station. Near the contra-dictions of stations everywhere: the rushing to and the rushing away from, the heaviness of machinery permitting the lightness of flight, the smiles of children next to the closed faces of adults.

In some cities the occasion of a person jumping into the path of an oncoming train would draw the media, but in Tokyo hundreds of rail suicides happen every year. And so, while travellers returning home will often comment, 'Another suicide on the tracks today', the event itself will not necessarily make the news. If it does, it is more often than not an opportunity for troubled railway officials to discuss the inconvenience it causes. To mention the fact that it takes about fifty minutes to resume schedules no matter how fast they work, and that every time someone chooses this method of death the railway is flooded with angry calls from delayed commuters. In one incident it took three hours to restore services because they were still searching for the head.

Various methods have been tried to deter would-be victims, including forcing next-of-kin to pay for property damage (the shame involved in incurring such a debt for the family being seen as possibly a greater deterrent than the costs themselves).

Now the railway is trying mirrors, since some psychologists have suggested that, should potential suicides catch sight of their own reflections, they might be brought back to a true realisation of what they are about to do. Picture it: the search for your one face in a mirror on the opposite side of the tracks, among all the other faces crowding the platform, all the charcoal suits, all the lives looking – from where you stand – uniformly controlled and grey; the consideration that perhaps there are not many faces but only one, and that you are merely a brief expression passing across it.

❦

A memory: Mr S., pausing at the slight rustle of my gown, sighing quietly.

'And you? Tell me how it is with you. Are you happy?'

'Yes, I am perfectly happy. Let us continue to speak of other things . . .'

'You have not yet told me where you come from.'

'Aren't you forgetting the purpose of our meetings? Have we not agreed that I am recently come from the ancient capital, Heian-Kyo, to this room, for you, so that we can travel back together, so that you can know it again in any way you choose?'

'It's only that I'm used to being in charge – of everything. This is slightly . . . unsettling. The screen. Just your voice and that scent in the air. If you could only tell me your real name.'

'My name is Sei Shōnagon.'

A short stop down the line from Omotosando is Shibuya, that great melting pot of Tokyo youth, the place that demands you allow yourself to be lost in a crowd without quite losing yourself – or at least without losing sight of what you came to buy.

Around Hatchiko Square everyone is looking for something, like the ghost of the dog after whom the square is named, who waited in vain for his dead master at the same place before the station exit, at the same time, for years.

The endless wave floods across the intersection and

recedes. A collective loss of self. The invisibility of a great number. Forward, back. Forward. A rhythm that could kill if conditions were slightly altered. If the traffic lights malfunctioned in a certain way (which, granted our efficiency, they will doubtless never do), if the earth shuddered more than usual on a typical day, and the road buckled . . .

A short way up from the station, kids in padded silver jackets are selling tomorrow's matchbox-sized phone-fax-computer-watch combos at unbeatable prices, and further up still, a man with an unglamorous red cross painted on a board stares uncertainly into the distance, waiting for offers of blood. The shoppers jostle past him, pallid, heavy-eyed, mouths half-open, looking as if they've given and forgotten in the same moment.

On Saturday evenings would-be escorts dressed in evening suits form a vaguely-threatening semi-circle around the station exit, and wait, and wait. While people inevitably surge towards them, no one is ever seen deliberately approaching the group or actually leaving with one of them. Certainly not the Japanese Shibuya girls with their freshened orange tans and their cowboy hats pushed far back on bleached hair. Suddenly one girl pauses to fish in a Prada handbag for a cigarette. Before she can adjust her slightly twisted kimono, the crowd charging out from the underground has swirled around her, has picked her up as though she were a piece of drift-wood, has carried her off in a totally new direction, one that she will later probably believe she has chosen herself.

This is Tokyo. Anything can happen here.

❦

I do not know what it is that is broken. Only that I slip in and out of a mental wakefulness that can't translate itself to speech, to movement. I know I should open my eyes to let them know I can hear. To let them know my mind is still alive. But something won't allow this to happen. It's like being in some advanced state of meditation, knowing your body is there, but also being disconnected from it.

I don't even know if you are still alive.

❦

It was my mother's family, generations ago, who began to sell incense from a fragrant wooden shop-front behind which the whole family lived and worked. Even the youngest children helped with grinding some of the ingredients, while the male head of the household supervised every process, at last sealing himself into a closed and shuttered room while he perfected a final blend according to the family's secret recipes. Many variables would affect the end product: the exact origin of the perfumed wood, the amount of sun it had received while growing, the way harvesting and moisture and storage had already affected the spices . . .

The result took several different forms. Perhaps most significantly there was the chipped mixture called Shokoh which would be placed on hot ash and burned on Buddhist altars, but there were other specialities too. Sometimes honey or plum might be added to the powdered ingredients, the whole thoroughly kneaded and then rolled into tiny balls to form *nerikoh*. The honey or plum maintained a perfect moist environment for the full development of the fragrance, after which the blend was aged for at least three years, the longer the better where ultimate quality was concerned. 'No possibility of hurrying it up,' my mother would say with a smile. That mixture, sealed in ceramic jars and buried in the damp earth, took exactly the time it needed. To our ancestors it was like making a deposit in the bank. But more than that, it was a part of themselves that grew in complexity and richness. Incense was a way of life. Then, as now, all the processes were carried out by hand – grinding, blending, kneading, rolling. A family business.

Another favourite was joss sticks, based on the ancient form which originated in India. They not only provided fragrance but could also be used to measure time, since the rate of burning was so predictable. In contrast to the Indian variety, the Japanese stick originated as solid incense with no central bamboo core. Up to fifteen different ingredients were used at once, including small quantities of the prized elements *jinkoh*, cloves and ambergris. The most common binding agent was the almost scentless bark of the Judas tree, valued because it would not upset the delicate balance of the chosen fragrances. Once the paste had achieved the right consistency it was pushed through a mould to emerge like thin spaghetti. The skill, my mother said, was all in the final grinding and blending, otherwise the sticks might warp or not burn well.

There were also *nioi-bakuro*, sachets of ground ingredients packed into little embroidered bags. Women would place them between folded linen or slip them into the sleeves of their kimono. Apart from their delicate scent, they were believed to repel bad luck.

'And do they really work?' I demanded of my mother one day after we had moved back to Japan, desperate to know if there was anything I could use to control fate.

Her eyes looked into mine as though searching for the future.

'It could be worse, couldn't it?' she said at last, hugging me and then spinning me around the kitchen in an impromptu dance, her sleeves flying out like scented wings, stretching to test the air for me.

My father was an American, teaching at a Tokyo university when he met my mother, a beautiful and committed student who initially refused to take him seriously. Their courtship began in the library, among a forest of hushed and ordered shelves. He said he fell in love with the crown of her head and her eyelashes first of all because, as a well-bred Japanese girl, she instinctively lowered her eyes when a man focused his attention on her. It didn't take my father long to realise that flirting was going to be a major obstacle in itself. He taught literature, wrote poetry, shocked the department where he was gaining a cautious acceptance by decorating his tie with poems and drawings in order to attract her attention since, if she looked his way at all, she would never manage to glance higher than his chest. He would watch her lips for the slightest hint of a smile at his efforts. When at last he saw it one day, he knew she was going to be his wife.

His own mother remained in something of a state of shock over the unexpected marriage, the honeymoon on a tiny island she couldn't even locate on a map and – eighteen months later – my birth. A couple of years later still, a job in New York drew my parents towards America, and for the first time my grandmother gazed anxiously into my face, seeking recognition of one of her own. I was judged quite a pretty little thing, with delicate ears. My mother, then, had not been a complete disaster.

If I could have foreseen how few years would be permitted me to share with my father, would I have wanted anything to be different? Apart from wishing for more hours in the day, I don't think so.

He died sprinting across a New York street one evening as a stolen car shot out of the darkness. What changed after that was my confidence in a universe whose laws I thought I had understood. I knew I had to reconsider every part of it then, but suddenly it was too full of emptiness for me to do anything but sit in my room and rock myself backwards and forwards, waiting for him to put his head around the door and grin at me and tell me it was just a trick and that I had every right to be angry with him. The last thing we did together was construct one of our handmade books, the new creamy-white pages for once in perfect alignment, waiting to be filled, scrap-book fashion, with the beautiful and imperfect fragments of a life.

Up until my father died, one of my certainties had been that it was enough for me to be me. And then the planets shifted and the balance of many things was destroyed. My mother and I had gone to stay at my grandparents' beach house in the Hamptons. One morning while my mother was still sleeping upstairs, my grandmother called me over to her large pink-patterned armchair. She lifted my chin and gazed into my eyes. 'I think,' she said slowly, turning me slightly towards the light as though examining a flawed piece of porcelain, 'we should be able to fix those ... quite easily.'

I have often relived the nights that followed, the way the vertical strip of light through my bedroom door seemed to expand and contract with the rise and fall of voices downstairs. Hearing my mother's quiet controlled tone alternate with my grandmother's confident drawl, a deeper and more persuasive sound, as pervasive a note as the perfume which dominated every room she entered. Remembering the way certain words lingered in the air: future ... acceptance ... school ... training ... acceptance ... acceptance.

At that time we walked a lot on the beach together, my mother and I. It must have occurred to her almost immediately, once the initial shock had been blunted by a sameness of days, that now we really were an aloneness of two; strangers in a way, to both the country we had left five years before and the one that now witnessed our loss. My parents together had been a bright – even exotic – cosmopolitan couple, a fresh breeze amongst the older, well-heeled members of my grandparents' set. Now my mother, still uncertain of the wisdom of returning to Japan, nevertheless realised how Japanese she felt in her emotional isolation – a Japanese woman alone with a child.

The feelings that my grandmother had suppressed while my father was still alive now surfaced more visibly every day. And the one thing that became clear was that I was kin (and could be made more so with considerable input and effort) whilst my mother was not.

The plan that emerged was for me to be raised in America. To have all the benefits that this could offer. To be sent, as soon as practicable, to a good boarding school where I could assimilate totally with the sort of people who would later be helpful to me.

I remember being in the hall at the height of the inevitable tension, my mother holding out her hand for me to take as we prepared to go out on a walk, my grandmother surging into view as if from nowhere, eyes wide and smiling, her voice rising with a false and terrible brightness, 'Why don't you stay in with me this afternoon, darling? I've bought some new clothes for you. We could try them on right here and now. Would you like that?' The slight hardness in her look as her eyes rose to challenge those of my mother: You do want the best for her, don't you? Would any mother not want her child to have every possible advantage?

My own uncertainty grew as I stood looking first at my mother's suspended, outstretched hand, and then at my grandmother's arms, suddenly thin and vulnerable, also reaching out for me. My child's mind swivelled faster and faster between the two of them, not wanting to hurt anybody, until the ground seemed to slant up at me from a crazy angle. Please, don't make me choose, don't make me choose! Until then it had been easy to put into practice what I had always been taught, the civilised norms of not doing damage, not being the cause of hurt to others. Until the moment I had to turn my back on my grandmother. In that instant, without realising it, I had accepted more than my mother's outstretched hand. I had decided my future. From that time on my grandmother avoided us as much as possible. It was made clear that she expected we would be planning a future that did not include her or her world. I think she somehow held my mother responsible for my father's death in the overall sense that had they never met, he might have still been alive. She needed to blame someone. Later I would dream of her standing on a cliff-top, turning round to me with the same desperate smile on her face, the arms still outstretched. She would open her mouth to speak, but the sound of the waves would always drown out her words and I would see only the brightly-painted mouth, its tiny lines softened over and over by nightly creams, opening and closing like that of a wounded animal.

I wonder now if anyone realised the depth of her grief over her son's death. Her façade was always too complete, a self-control that must have snapped into place automatically and forestalled any suggestion of help or pity from others. It was years before I found a way to penetrate the memory of her coldness and understand it. I was growing up in Japan by then, noticing all those composed faces with their troubled eyes, sensing the aura of privacy that surrounded individuals like armour.

My retired-diplomat grandfather had been so much easier to love – a gentle, softly-spoken person who deliberately dressed down in a somewhat rumpled way, and was more at home with a book or trowel than with the socially prominent group of New Yorkers his wife spoke of as friends. I had the impression that there was an instinctive empathy between my mother and grand-father and that he would have done anything he could to avoid hurting her. During what became the almost daily discussions about my future he was usually tact-fully absent, out on some vital mission involving twine for a new climbing plant or paper clips for his desk or even toffees, because 'all children like toffees, cheers them up'. He was not to outlive his son by more than a year, but we could not have known that the last time we saw him, pressing a newly-cut camellia into my mother's hand through the open window of our taxi.

The only other relative I knew about on my father's side was his elder sister who had totally rejected her mother's lifestyle and gone off to study tropical medicine in South America. My grandmother would lift her daughter's occasional letter from the morning pile and hold it up between thumb and forefinger for a long while, as though premature opening might release some unidentified winged creature that would aim straight for her and start burrowing into her flesh.

And so, at the age of seven, I came to live in the home of my mother's elder brother. For a Japanese house it was large, although to me it seemed relatively smallish, cold and darkly intimidating after the brightly-lit, centrally heated homes of America. Before all else, it smelt so different. The slightly wheaty odour of the *tatami* matting in each room, the pungency of black beans and dried fish in the kitchen, the acrid sting of my uncle's cigarette smoke that caught in my throat and made my eyes water.

My mother and I were to share a room at the back of the house. As we knelt to unroll our futons on that first night I caught a strange look on her face, a frightened, uncertain expression. 'It's nothing,' she said, noticing that I had stopped and was watching her. 'Just for a moment I felt as though none of it had happened: marriage, America – the three of us –' She paused and rested her hands on her knees. As I sat there, staring at her across the futon in the failing light, I had the sense that something was shrinking within her. I reached out to touch her arm, needing quickly, urgently, to break the silence that was becoming darkness itself. 'I'm here,' I said, as loudly as I dared. 'I'm here.'

For the first few weeks I was in a state of culture shock, not helped by the stern looks of disapproval thrown my way every time I encountered my silent and stony-faced uncle. It was shortly made clear to me that all the faults I had acquired in the US would have to be rectified as soon as possible. My speech was too loud, my deportment totally unsuited to a young girl, and I had the outrageous habit of asking questions whenever the mood took me. The stilted way in which he had greeted us at the airport suggested that my parents' marriage had been as unwelcome to my uncle as it had been to my paternal grandmother, but he was a wealthy man and family pride was a serious consideration. Provided I remained under his roof I would receive the best possible education, in the first instance via several private tutors who would try to make up for the 'deficiencies' of my previous education as quickly as possible. Later there might be cooking and flower arranging, perhaps trips to some famous temples – we would see ...

I did not at first realise that the one bitter regret my uncle had at not marrying was the absence of an heir, not only someone who would inherit his wealth, but who could also be trained by him to appreciate his one true passion in life – the art of the sword. I suppose it was a significant disappointment to him to suddenly have a girl in his care, in place of a more valued boy (and not even fully-Japanese, as his occasional careless remarks so acutely reminded me) but nevertheless I was a child who could be instructed, and who would thus placate one of the unfulfilled desires of his life – the need to instruct. Therefore, twice a week after entering my uncle's house, I began to receive formal lectures from him about the Japanese sword and its importance in the samurai-warrior tradition. In order to encourage my enthusiasm for the subject he also provided a book of sombre black-and-white photographs with Japanese captions. Unfortunately for my studies, my curiosity was only piqued by the sword pictures if I could make something else appear out of the image on the page. I found that if I half-closed my eyes, the central positive sword shape would transform itself into a negative chasm, and then the dark background on either side of it would become two sheer walls of rock – a strange landscape where one could wander forever without being found.

There were many new rules to learn about my uncle's house. Being a restorer of antiques, he had acquired a number of precious objects for his own collection, but they were sparingly displayed. Even so, I was warned not to touch anything. Not the worm-riddled warriors that stood guard inside the front door as though to interrogate hapless visitors, not the stiff scroll painting of a gnarled tree that hung in the passageway, and certainly not the formal flower arrangement that was delivered each Saturday by a man in a white coat, with all the solemnity of a surgeon engaged in a heart transplant. I lived in constant fear of tripping on the *tatami* one day, and falling through one of the flimsy paper *shoji* screens, which of course would only be the first incident of a chain reaction . . . I grew to expect constant reprimands from my uncle, and even found a certain advantage in this: if he was criticising me, it usually meant I was drawing fire away from my mother.

Soon after we arrived in Japan I asked my mother if we could go together to visit *The Bridge of Dreams*, the family incense business she had inherited and whose history I knew by heart. It was a trip that was repeatedly planned and then cancelled, like so many, by my uncle's indirect intervention. When I timidly mentioned incense to him as a possible topic of conversation we could share, he snapped back that he only thought of it in connection with joss sticks burning on family altars to commemorate the dead.

Although for reasons of practicality the incense shop had been managed by someone else for many years, it remained a family constant, a symbol to bring my mother's parents comfort in difficult or stressful times. This is what our ancestors did, this is how they enhanced life. We too could someday do this again, and re-forge our links with a noble tradition. Marriage and life in America had largely prevented my mother from involving herself in the business at any level. One day I hoped it would be a force for good in our lives. A way of entering a Japan that I had only known through my imagination.

I was so preoccupied by my own daily problems that it took me a little while to realise how much my mother's behaviour had changed since our return to Japan. Was it an intensifying of her sense of loss, caused by memories of the early days of her marriage? Or an instinctive return, in her brother's house, to the earlier days of her more vulnerable adolescence? I remember the time she had delighted in showing me a nest of young birds in a New England tree, and how we had later together drawn the *kanji* for 'learn' which literally means 'to fly by your own wings'. Her own parents had died just as she was entering university and it seemed that she had only truly gained her freedom – become her own person – during her university years, away from home and the influence of her ambitious and domineering brother.

I found myself shivering sometimes, just thinking about who my mother might have married if she had not, by miraculous chance, met my father. What would that other child – those other children, perhaps – have been like? Would I have existed, but in a different body? No, because half of that person would have been completely other . . . The terrifying element of chance. Of life. Of death.

I had asked my grandmother about death once, when a cat had been run over outside their house. She looked puzzled for a moment, interrupted in the writing of invitations, and let out a small sigh. 'Well, it's . . . when you just . . . stop breathing. Like the little cat – it's not in any pain – you don't have to worry about it suffering. It's just . . . stopped breathing, that's all.' And then she added absentmindedly, 'And its soul has gone to Heaven – Animal Heaven, of course.' I tried to imagine what that would be like, the moment when I would stop breathing. I tried holding my breath and it was terrifying. I couldn't do that forever after I was dead! I started to panic. My grandfather gave the matter longer and more considered attention while we pruned the apple trees together – he asking my approval as to the next cut and I gravely giving the go-ahead. He said it was really nothing at all like holding your breath. Nothing At All. More like going into a different room in a very large house. Your family and friends (who were living) were in one big room, and you were in another. So even though you couldn't see each other through the walls, they'd know that you were still there (in all the ways that mattered) and vice versa. Certainly nothing would alter how everyone thought and felt about their loved ones, and that was the most important thing, didn't I think? I needed some time to digest the large-house-with-all-the-rooms idea, which raised all sorts of other questions, although I felt I had quite enough to deal with over the death issue in the first instance. And it did, in some way I couldn't define, have a certain logic − at least as reasonable as tigers running around a tree and turning into melted butter, which I had accepted far more quickly, although I'd been younger at the time and therefore less critical.

I knew my father had always encouraged my mother's love of painting, and it had been one of her great pleasures to go to New York galleries and museums, taking me with her from an early age, to explore the world through new eyes. At the same time as I was learning nursery rhymes, I was seeing the way Matisse danced with colour and the way Van Gogh threw it into the air to become the sun. I floated over O'Keeffe deserts and dived head-first into Frankenthaler abstraction. I went on foraging trips with everyone from Hals to Hockney and in the process learned that painting was as natural to life as breathing. I still have the paper-cuts that my mother and I would set to making when the mood took us, decorating whichever surface seemed most likely to shock and delight my father when he came through the door, jaded by department politics and students passing off essays-to-please as original thought.

The habits of daily life in America seemed to slip away from us like water running through open hands. Ultimately we became absorbed into the pattern of life in my uncle's spartan household almost without realising it. Despite his wealth, he economised wherever possible. A modest cleaning lady was his only luxury, and by the time we had recognised the sound of her discreet activities she had nearly always disappeared. At least I had my various lessons, provided by several tutors, to keep my mind distracted from our uneventful domestic routine for a good part of the week. My mother on the other hand, had taken over the shopping and the preparation of meals and in some curious way my uncle managed to inhibit any activity of hers that was not connected with these things, or at least with the smooth running of the household. Were she to plan an excursion he would discover some account that needed paying in person or some bureaucratic matter requiring family representation. If she sat down to read a book he would suddenly remember that he had run out of liniment for his aching leg muscles or antacid for his indigestion. Little by little she grew more self-contained and the uncertainty in her eyes I had seen there on that first evening grew to become part of her normal expression. From time to time she would gather herself together and then she would draw me to her and whisper long into the night while she stroked my hair, telling me not to forget all the things my father had taught me, not to forget what he had stood for, not to forget him. And then she would take something to help her sleep, a sachet of powdered sedative, and after that she would sleep as deeply as she once had naturally in America.

'Unbreakability, rigidity and cutting power,' my uncle would stress, walking the length of the room while one hand beat down like a dull blade itself into the palm of the other. By the time I had been under his roof for a month I knew about the absolute importance of the different layers of sword metal – the soft and durable core enveloped by its repeatedly forged outer layer, the thickness and strength of one side of the blade compared to the thinness and cutting ability of the other. The way the extreme edge of that other must be expertly tempered separately from the rest of the metal using a special heat-resistant clay to shield the bulk of the blade, and the way in which that enabled the creation of a master sword with a supreme cutting edge.

'The finest swords are those with a name. Can you tell me the names of those held to be the greatest sword-makers?'

An ambulance siren sounded in the long silence that followed this question, as my eye traced a strip of binding on the *tatami* mat in front of me. The bulk of my uncle loomed up before me as he stood with his back to the window, blocking off the light.

'What, then, is the meaning of the sword to a samurai?'

I breathed a small sigh of relief.

'The sword is the soul of the samurai.'

'When did the "Old Sword Period" finish?'

'At . . . at the end of . . .'

'At the end of the sixteenth century. Now we will *reapply* ourselves to the five traditions of the Old Sword Period. You seem to have been having trouble distinguishing one from the other.

'To begin once more: the Bizen Tradition – named for the Bizen Province in the region of the Inland Sea – produced three great names among the smiths of the late Heian period – pay close attention please! . . .'

And so it would continue, the odour of stale tobacco, the monotone voice droning into my ears with dates, facts and a limitless admiration for the qualities of forged metal, and what they represented.

There was another room to the right of the one in which I received my lessons on sword etiquette and history. I knew with absolute certainty that I must never set foot in this space, my uncle's inner sanctum. One day, however, I had a chance to glimpse the interior through a gap in the sliding screen that divided the room from the passage. Rows of books, two antique swords hanging on the wall, a suit of leather armour in a glass case, the helmet on a shelf of its own like the sightless head of some mythical beast. I had been on the point of tip-toeing away after noting these things when I briefly caught sight of someone moving across the room and pausing in front of a mirror. My heart missed a beat – he looked as though he had stepped straight from the pages of one of my history books. Then, as he muttered a few words to himself, I almost laughed out loud. It was the ultimate caricature – my uncle dressed as a sword-bearing warrior, a stout, would-be defender of all that had been lost to the past.

My mother's sadness did not pass with time. If anything it grew worse, sometimes seeming to transform itself into a series of small accidents of self-hurt – fingers too often cut on knives or paper, boiling water spilt on a foot or hand, an arm carelessly touching an iron, as though she were trying to punish herself for the indulgence that was sadness. Or was it for the indulgence of still being alive?

It was then that I first came up with the idea of a diary, of writing down for my mother, in English, a private collection of thoughts, memories and stories that might interest her in life again. Did I also think that if I could recreate a familiar world on a page that it might make my life right again too?

To begin with I wrote about the good times we had shared in America. The first kimono she had secretly ordered for me from Japan. When I opened my eyes and saw it draped over a chair I thought it was a plain robe on to which someone had scattered some of the spring blossom that was arranged in a vase in our hall. The surge of joy when I touched the silken surface and found it covered with a shower of embroidered petals, and then the sensation of smooth coolness as the fabric enveloped my warm skin. I felt my arms reach up and out for a moment, like fine branches. I felt strong and beautiful on that day. I remembered too – how could my mother have known so exactly? – when we waited together one summer evening by a branch from which a chrysalis hung. At a certain moment the breeze dropped but the slender casing continued to move. And, as though we were willing this with our focused gaze, it started to open. In a hushed voice she told me, 'Quickly, hold out your finger.' The wings unfolded then, like a sudden rose – such newness . . . and without a pause the butterfly crawled on to my finger as to some island of safety, and sat there as I hardly dared breathe, its wings moving backwards and forwards in the warm air, feeling their way towards wonderful things.

I wrote at night, under the bedclothes by torch-light. English had become my secret vice by now. I ached to hear it spoken again, since my uncle had decreed that all communication should be in Japanese. He had decided that the only way I would catch up with my peers was to adopt the 'immersion method' of language instruction, and while there was obviously some point to this, it initially enclosed me in a world where I constantly doubted my ability to express myself correctly. There were days when I counted myself lucky to have understood half of what had been said, a situation that uncharacteristically for me seemed to inhibit rather than encourage the asking of questions. The only neighbours I saw were people of my uncle's age – no children – and so the normal friendships, that should have provided a pleasurable path to assimilation, were nothing more to me than wistful imaginings. Although we were technically in one of the outer suburbs of Greater Tokyo, the cosmopolitan centre, with its mad clash of cultures and casual transformation of any foreign influence, was another world away. My knowledge of life in Japan therefore, came to be based more and more on the tightly-structured norms of my uncle's household with its emphasis on unquestioning obedience and restraint.

Later I would see in these months the gradual ebbing away of my childhood self even as I was trying to hold on to the best of it through memory. I wrote about my 'other' life half in fear that it too would slip away, needing to confirm its substance, its validity.

I gave my first written offerings to my mother, in the form of a small hand-sewn book. She sat down under a tree in the garden and opened it carefully. I watched her as she read, one arm held still across her body as though to remind herself that emotion was a private experience that should never again be publicly revealed. She pressed the book between the palms of her hands when she had finished reading it, and when she raised her head her smile seemed to light her face from within. 'You are my little Sei Shōnagon,' she said. And then she briefly became her old self again, telling me a story in turn, a glimpse into tenth-century Japan and a lady of the Heian court – Sei Shōnagon, whose diary preserved her life and times for centuries, on a chance gift of paper from the Empress.

It was to be many years before I would again be referred to as 'Sei Shōnagon' and by then, like my namesake, I too would have acquired a background in the study of the noble arts: poetry, calligraphy, brush-painting – and survival.

Everything has its rituals. Even the weaving of dreams.

Mr S. has been coming to see me for a long time, ever since his premature retirement. In the beginning, the only need, to escape:

'I feel old today, just suddenly – today. That was the thought that woke me up. A mind as old as its body. It's as though it happened overnight, this clicking into place of something I've only ever viewed as a distant potential – the unwanted combination to a safe where I thought I could lock up Time.

'Now I need to be with someone. I need not to be alone. I think you are the only companion I could speak to about such things. So many unwritten rules in ordinary life, preventing the saying of anything that really matters. As though every good, spontaneous thing about us has to be crushed.

'Take me away with you, again, take me away from Tokyo, to the other place . . .'

'Close your eyes and we will go out into the garden. It is after dawn. Late into the hour of the tiger.

'We can see the lake from where we are standing, and the pine island in the middle. The morning light is just starting to spread across the stream that winds through the garden and around the building. The inner blends with the outer here, almost seamlessly. What grows in profusion outside is often painted and embroidered inside. Thus rooms are named for the flowers they overlook. As it has always been, we are more concerned with diversion than with protecting ourselves from elements we know we cannot control. The curtain, the shutter, is just a temporary gesture to night – a leaf across the mouth of the burrow.

'The earth is beginning to stir. In the distance there

are geese, flying towards the temples of the great mountain range of Hiei. A faint mist gives way to a fresher coolness that brings with it the sound of the geese, the scent of the pine . . .'

'Tell me what you are wearing.'

'Beneath a Chinese jacket, unlined silk robes – many of them – in the muted colours of morning, pale blues and dove greys and soft pinks woven with a hair-thin thread of gold so that they are slightly luminous. A layered sky. At the edges of the sleeves the colours overlap – a quiet rainbow spreading back from the wrists.'

'And your hair?'

'My hair is long – black and shining. When I turn suddenly it makes a single curve, folding itself like a wing against the blue silk of my robe. When it is combed I close my eyes and feel it move like a river, full of its own inner light.'

'And your hands?'

'My hands are small and pale. Small, smooth, white hands that are the symbol of both prison and privilege. Whiter still in the moonlight when I pick up a brush and hesitate over my paper, listening to the night.'

'What paper have you chosen?'

'In terms of its whiteness something akin to Moon Palace Calligraphy, although the one I have reached for on this occasion is thicker and far more complex. I have an extraordinary choice. The papers here are beautiful beyond belief. They are a part of our intimacy, a texture appropriate for every mood, every slight alteration of a season. Love can spring from the message sent by the paper alone, the world enclosing the words. See the letter for a moment – tied in the customary knot, untied hastily and read with quick bright movements of the eye. Later, held to the lips, pressed inside a kimono, it becomes the first exploration of a lover's hand, the first skin exchange of warmth.'

Sometimes I almost forget that it all began with Mr S. I had known his daughter as a fellow student at a painting class I attended. Initially we had drawn closer as friends when she confided in me about the loss of her mother. And then one day, the story of her father emerged.

'They had the habit of talking together late into the night at the kitchen table, long after he had made it home from the office. It didn't matter how late he got in, she'd be there with a bowl of hot noodles, even a flower in a separate little hollow of his chopstick rest. They'd shared so much together they were more like one quietly-organised person than two – a real "mandarin-duck couple", in it for the long haul. I suppose that's almost a rarity these days. It seems like everyone I know has someone in the family who's just split up or is planning to, or who would like to if it weren't for the children. Of course it was an arranged marriage, like so many then, but my mother once told me that they'd seen each other long before the introduction, when they were both quite young, and that she knew something had been exchanged – perhaps even decided – in one long shy look between them.

'So, after all those years, she was still the one he went to for comfort and advice, the one who could give him some perspective on life. And no matter how long it took she would always come up with something, perhaps just a small thing, but it would usually be enough, as a pinpoint of light at the end of a tunnel is enough to indicate the way ahead. He could sleep like a baby, as long as he could sort out the day in his mind before putting his head on the pillow. I don't know – was it her understanding, or just her calmness that helped him? I'm not like that. I'm more like him. I get exasperated too easily.

'It's been over a year since she died and it's more than depression for him now. I hardly know how to tell you the rest . . .

'He was at Shinjuku. It happened at Shinjuku station on a Friday evening.

'His superiors had asked if they could "have a word". There was the likelihood of a company merger, they said. The need for certain inevitable measures – voluntary redundancy in a number of cases – and they had good news: the package was extremely generous, more than generous. They were sure that he would be one of the first to offer to step down, after all he no longer had a wife or young family to support. I suppose they told themselves they were being helpful, giving him the maximum amount of time to prepare.

'The others tried to cheer him up in the standard way, wanting to take him out for drinks and so forth. He's always hated those endless binges but he's gone along with them in the past because obviously there's no choice if you work in a company. But this time he said no, he felt like getting home and thinking things through. Another colleague had left earlier to go to an appointment and saw my father at the station, saw his trance-like eyes and his face as rigid as a corpse. The friend said he hardly thought about the decision to keep a few paces behind, it just seemed the only thing to do.

'My father kept walking, staring straight ahead. He walked to the end of the platform where the trains arrive, and then he suddenly did a right turn, like a soldier obeying an order, and walked to the edge just as the warning signal sounded. If his friend had not been there . . . He made out it must have been his fault my father went so close to the edge, bowing and apologising as he pulled him back. Then he saw him home and called me.

'I feel as though I've failed my father but I can't get him to talk to me. I've tried everything. Perhaps it's because he's ashamed of showing weakness. He knows that I know everything. He was always so proud of his position – virtually gave his life to the company – and now he's seeing himself as one step away from destitution, leaving his shoes outside a cardboard box at night. You know there are unemployed company directors doing that in Shinjuku Central Park? And bowing to the person in the next box at exactly the angle they deem appropriate to the situation. When was it we decided obedience to the rules would solve everything? Or was it so instilled in us from the beginning that we just couldn't break the habit? No wonder the young are going crazy.'

Mr S., you should understand, would not have felt capable of speaking to me face-to-face about anything of deeply personal significance. The social constraints would have made such a meeting stilted, perhaps even hostile. And so his daughter and I invented a harmless fantasy. He was told that I had a private reason for guarding my anonymity and for that reason there would be a screen between us during our meetings, in the manner of the women of the Heian period, entertaining their male guests.

More recently Mr S. has found a partial way of rebuilding his life – teaching calligraphy. He is busier than he thought possible, teaching, not traditionally-minded Japanese students as he imagined he would, but foreigners – *gaijin* – from all over the world, who are fascinated by the movement in a painted line, the music in a brushstroke. He can't believe so much has changed since his own student days.

He muses aloud for some time as we sit in the quiet room, incense moving imperceptibly between us.

'Is it only through foreigners it will continue? Hard to believe that the traditions were so recently guarded by keeping the gates firmly locked, the barbarians out. Now it seems that the only hope is to offer our past to anyone who can see why it is worth preserving.

'Listen to this: I went to buy a new brush and a certain ink stick with a light in it like dawn moving across dark water. I went to a shop that has a floor specialising in such materials, and the girl serving me said, "But why don't you try one of these?" And she handed me an acrylic fibre pen with a liquid at one end ready to be squirted down on to the brush. No careful grinding of the ink to release all those subtle hues and shadings, its capacity for making something live on paper. She said everyone uses these now – less messy. And so quick! And so quick. What is it they think they are rushing towards?'

History and literature were what we most often spoke about together. His greatest enthusiasm was reserved for the Heian period – ranging from the eighth to the twelfth century – and what saddened him was that so many things about that time were lost or unknown and were likely to remain so forever. Like me he had read the poetry and diaries and other literature of the age, but all of it a long time ago, before company work had taken over his life. And so he would sometimes ask me to remind him of the details, to speak as one of them as if in a play, as though I too had sprung from the pages of the ancient books, wearing the robes of the old nobility, spending my days hidden behind fan and screen, my senses so attuned to my world that I could read a name in a footfall, a thought in the rap of a fan on a shutter. This is how I once again came to be called Sei Shōnagon after the author of *Makura no Soshi*, known in English as *The Pillow Book*.

We spoke of painting, of literature, of poetry. The way in which a prolonged period of peace allowed these things to flourish. The lavish attention paid to the staging of poetry competitions which took many forms, but were here (rare in our history), battles that no one truly lost. We also developed our own form of poetry competition, taking turns to provide the first line of a haiku which the other would complete.

In December he suggested,

Winter morning –

And I, remembering my five-year-old self in New England, offered:

shocked to greater whiteness by a robin.

In April I would propose,

Shoji –

opening with a small sigh

And he would conclude,

on listening blossom.

But we continued as we had begun, with the discretion of a paper screen between us. In all the time of this quietly developing friendship, we never once saw each other's faces.

An incense shop. A bridge to the past. Such an enterprise is nowadays a rarity, even in a major city that overflows with small businesses. Were you to ask the average Tokyoite about incense, you would probably be referred to any one of the major department stores. There, a smiling, immaculately-groomed assistant would direct you to one of the higher floors, to a corner display behind the traditional ceramics and kimono, where a few artfully-wrapped boxes of incense sticks and a handful of scented brocade bags would be scattered amongst the origami birds and handmade cards. In recent years incense has become a newly-discovered passion for some. For others it remains a memory that perfumes the collective unconscious, an aroma of the history that loosely binds us all.

The incense business that passed to me from my uncle's temporary guardianship in my last year of university filled me with conflicting feelings. On the one hand it was likely to provide me with a reasonable income and would therefore ensure my economic independence. On the other hand it brought my mother's stories suddenly and vividly to life and, with them, a reminder of almost unbearable grief. On the day I took possession of the shop my legacy seemed to me both tangible and intangible: on the one hand the narrow building with its neat shelving and carefully prepared stock; on the other, the scents, escaping all order, rising from the lower floor to the upper like overlapping dreams, or an unfinished poem.

For the privileged and powerful of Heian Japan, no art forms commanded more respect than music, the creation of gardens, and poetry. What could be more charming, therefore, than that the men of the court should observe their ladies flitting like bright birds through the beautifully composed gardens of the age, watching them murmuring amidst the peonies, laughing with a sound as bright as water splashing on stone? What could be more delightful than watching them picking up their instruments, their pens?

The leisure to play: some would say a path leading to creativity or decadence. Some would also say that certain well-placed women of the ancient capital Heian Kyo (later the site of Kyoto) excelled at both. The court not only sanctioned but actively encouraged the perfection of brushwork and literary composition. Such accomplishments were as much prized as any other a man might seek in a spouse or concubine. And what harm could it do for ladies to write in the Japanese or 'female script' – *katakana* – which allowed such relative fluidity of expression, instead of the more formal *kanji* used by men on all occasions of importance?

Among the host of women who wrote in *katakana* during this time: Fujiwara Michitsuna no Haha, author of the highly individual and revealing *Kagero Diary*; Murasaki Shikibu, diarist and author of what is perhaps the most significant work of Japanese literature, *The Tale of Genji*; the great poet and diarist Izumi Shikibu; Sugawara Takasue no Musume, author of the *Sarashina Diary* and *The Tale of Hamamatsu Chunagon*, a fabulous story of dreams, reincarnation and bizarre adventure; and Sei Shōnagon who was one day given a quantity of fine paper by the Empress, and who began, with the thought, 'In Spring, it is the dawn that is the most beautiful', to compose her *Pillow Book*.

The luxury to write. The time to spend an afternoon choosing a fragrance with which to scent a new garment. The freedom to love (discreetly) at will. These lying jaggedly alongside the inability to walk out of the gate and down the road, the inappropriateness of cooking one's own meal, the impossibility of spending a day unattended.

When there is so much absurdity you cannot change, so many polite rules and petty restrictions to navigate wisely if you are to survive, you must work within a framework, you must work with the materials to hand. Take up a brush in the tenth century and, with an innocent smile on your lips, begin by providing your world with a picture it will want to embrace. A picture of itself. A picture of you. And all the while you are doing this, the tip of your brush will be easing under the door of your cage, edging it open, little by little, until you can escape and fly – if not far outside your garden, then at least over it – and from there you can observe all its wonderful and dreadful detail (of which you cannot help but be a part) and when the time is right, and they have forgotten you for a moment, you can swoop down and pluck the essence from the history of your age and save it so that later, much later, what you saw and felt and lived will be known.

Over and over again I return to that most recent period – the time of the perfumed room above the incense shop where what began as a social diversion to assist a friend's father continued as a form of private salon, an echo of the meetings between male visitors and the women of the Heian court, who could speak to each other with remarkable frankness provided the conventions were observed. A screen was all-important. Behind it, a female courtier could receive visitors and news of the outside world; it enlarged her universe at the same time as it concealed her, it preserved a required modesty even as it granted her extraordinary liberty.

One visitor came to see me at a time, initially to discuss our history and the arts, in a spirit of friendship. That was all. Speaking in the intimacy of a dimly-lit room, to a woman who existed as a voice – as words and silences. It seemed an easy matter for the conversation to veer towards the personal more often than not. Increasingly I began to encounter those whose private lives were drifting off course. The human need to speak, before the unspoken begins to destroy you from within. The equally overwhelming need for anonymity and utter discretion. Having begun, I continued, as much for my needs as for theirs.

Mr T.'s wife and child left him suddenly. Maybe it was the overtime – so much of it he would now and again lose track of whole weeks and only realise with a shock that a season was changing when he saw some mention of it on television. He'd fantasised about a house, one day, maybe – much farther out, of course, but still, a house . . . So there was work, with short breaks in between for travel and sleep. Sometimes he thought it would have been more practical to have kept a futon rolled up under his desk to have saved all those hours commuting on the train. And then, after the pressure of the week there was the inevitable need to release the tension.

He would pass out in a bar somewhere in Roppongi late on a Friday night and get home in the small hours of Saturday morning supported by a friend who was equally drunk, both of them smelling of vomit from the train. Nothing unusual in that, everyone did it.

Women were supposed to understand, but they'd changed so much since his mother's time. He blamed magazines and imported American TV – Japanese channels should be ashamed of themselves: *Star Trek* maybe, but *Sex and the City*? Anyone could see the world was headed for trouble.

He tried to keep his emotions in check as was normal, as he'd always been trained to do, but the sense of pointlessness, of rage at the stupidity of his one finite disappearing life overwhelmed him sometimes, usually just when he most needed to connect with another human being. He couldn't help yelling now and again. If he didn't he thought he could easily go mad – saw himself slipping sideways into a *manga*, a comic-book world of mutilation and destruction – with one single careless step. But he could hardly let his feelings show at the office. The sliver of time at home was where it – he – fell apart. His life was composed of corridors designed by someone else, for the benefit of someone else. Even his home was a narrow functional space with unspoken rules governing every feature of life within. At night he dreamt of being in a tunnel, of blue-black veins standing out all over his head, of the tension building inside him until they burst and the blood ran down over his outstretched hands like rain.

His daughter had developed a stutter, and his wife just crept round and round their tiny apartment dabbing at things as though she could clean up the mess of their lives if she worked at the veneered surfaces long enough. One night he had come home to find their immaculately, painfully tidy home empty, with a note on the kitchen table. It contained the polite phrases and excuses one might give a long-standing employer whose work environment one could no longer tolerate. She had even thought to include instructions for heating up his evening meal. The silence, the stillness in the air, covered his heart like a cold hand, and stayed there.

He grew obsessed with his apparent lack of understanding of the female psyche. How *did* they think? What made them happy? If only he could understand their minds the way he could analyse a computer program. Or find a manual that could lay it all out for him logically.

'I want to know something more about you, Sei Shōnagon. Are you from Tokyo?'

'Do you think you will know more about who I am by knowing where I come from? Besides, your question is flawed. Everyone in Tokyo comes from somewhere else. Isn't that what makes it what it is – what it isn't? I had hoped the anonymity provided by my screen would have encouraged a certain trust between us, rendering the usual social exchanges unnecessary.'

'You have no answers to my most important questions – ever.'

'Perhaps we could talk about your week. What has been going through your mind?'

'Nothing in particular. Everything.

'I spend nearly four hours on the train every day. At night I even dream about it. I watch people endlessly;

people through a forest of other people, imagining sudden twists of fate, great and extraordinary loves, unbelievable adventures. I don't know what I am really seeing when I look at all those silently rocking faces, people so folded into themselves, taking up the smallest possible space – all the learned habits of a lifetime. Stacked like origami in a box. Mostly I watch them cat-napping. Blank faces. Eyes closed. A slight rocking. Only a faint compression of the lips, a small furrow between the brows to indicate worry – job, money, family, maybe all three. Often the nap slides into sleep and the traveller begins to lean dangerously to one side or the other. Or two people side by side will start to slope towards each other, while those around keep glancing at them, fascinated to see what will happen with each jolt of the wheels. Now and again, several people will list in the same direction, like some half-dead chorus-line, drifting through their paces in slow motion. Most come back to consciousness with the same small jerk of the head, and look up and around to feign sudden alertness, although there's no one to impress. We're all strangers on a train. Even if we saw each other every day, we'd still be strangers and so we wouldn't count.

'I can't believe this is my life. It's unendurable. I'm sorry. I didn't intend to use our time like this . . .'

'You don't have to impress me. It's impressive enough to go out there every day and survive it.'

A sense of rising panic – a bird fluttering inside the uniform, dress, kimono – is instinctively followed, not by an urge to address the problem, but by a need to quell the emotion, to present the calm façade that will not disturb others. We are taught this unobtrusive behaviour at an early age, by example and by the thousand other forms of cultural osmosis that go towards shaping us.

The news reports that a missing schoolgirl has been found, nine years after she was abducted as a child. At eighteen she has spent half her life as a prisoner in an upstairs room of a suburban house in which the kidnapper's mother also lived. The victim never once left the floor where she was being held, and in all that time the mother had no idea – heard nothing – that would indicate there was a young girl in the house. The mother said she was afraid of her son, too afraid even to venture upstairs into his domain, and the girl, on being asked why she never tried to escape, said she also was afraid.

How much really lies hidden behind our carefully-drawn certainties, beyond our clean streets, our public façade of smooth mutual co-operation? You will not find out by trying to read faces in the quick surreptitious glances that are acceptable between passing strangers. You must look into the eyes to read other people's pain or misery. And it is not the custom to do that. Not here. It is the ultimate breach of etiquette.

Traditionally ours is a culture of self-discipline and self-restraint. Even during childbirth women are expected to remain silent – in control. When the dam bursts it does so properly, and at times for what would appear to be appallingly trivial reasons. A girl is stabbed to death on the way to school by a would-be boyfriend in whom she has shown no interest. A child is strangled near a temple well because her mother was not sufficiently friendly towards the strangler, another mother whose child attended the same kindergarten. A woman lured into 'Internet dating' is left to freeze to death after being chloroformed and robbed of a pathetically small sum of money. Recently one victim of jealousy was found in several prefectures, in segments. Behind the mask of non-feeling there is madness and passion and blood enough to rival any of the ancient myths.

My mother's restlessness continued after our return to Japan, for one year that almost seamlessly became two. During this period we were notified, via a brief, clipped message from my American grandmother, that my grandfather had died. My mother spent hours composing a letter to her mother-in-law, but received no reply. A few months after this I noticed that my mother had stopped taking an interest in the post at all, even refusing to open the progressively infrequent notes from her old New York friends. Their reality must have seemed light years away from hers. She told me one day that she thought their stories and banter cruel – were they trying to mock her? There were what I would later think of as periods of remission in my mother's growing depression, times when we shared laughter and stories, when she seemed like her old self. But all the while, steadily and surely, she was being drawn back into a cocoon, back into the role of submissive younger sister to my uncle. Although he continued to pay for the cleaning lady, he had expressed the wish that my mother herself prepare all his meals and he would creep silently into the kitchen while she was washing rice or slicing chicken to tell her exactly what she was doing wrong. I can still see him standing there in the doorway, his square head on its short thick neck, the eyes fixed unblinkingly on her like a tortoise surveying an obstacle.

Evenings in the hospital.

I can hear people talking in the corridor outside; the same ones I have heard before. They must come during the evening visiting hours. The subject of their conversation, I have pieced together, is an elderly lady – somebody's mother, somebody's grandmother. An operation to repair a broken hip and now, the laboured breathing that could be the early days of broncho-pneumonia.

'But what if she recovers?' a female voice is asking. (The 'what if' chilling me with its ruthless precision.) 'Who will look after her all day? And then the nights ... I can't just take time off. If you knew how completely my days have to be planned, down to the last second ...'

The man's voice is cautious: 'But surely you have enough seniority to take a few days, if necessary, just to help get her settled in – well, only if you wanted to, if you thought that was best. My idea was for us to take turns for a while. There again, there must be local nursing services, I suppose.'

'The only reason I'm still where I am is because I've conducted my professional life like a man. One slip and they'll find a way to get rid of me, and then all the years, all the discipline will be for nothing. Even the other women there would be glad to see me go. I've separated myself so completely from the "Office Lady" ideal that I'm a permanent object of suspicion, even hated in a bad week.'

She sounds very alone, the woman who is not an Office Lady. She has risen above being one of the vast army who anonymously maintain the smooth running of corporations throughout the country, whose job title hints as much at what is absent from such a life, as what is present. These days there is even a sub-species – the 'Office Flower'. Like butterflies, OFs live long enough – to make tea, sort and file, answer the phone and generally decorate the outer office. And then, just as suddenly as they arrived with their pleasing smiles and praiseworthy inoffensiveness, they are gone, married and off to the suburbs, wedded sometimes to colleagues in junior management (but preferably to someone older and significantly wealthier) and dispatched to rule at last over an office of their own – a home. The job, therefore, is also a bridge between those two divided female worlds, student life and motherhood, a narrow bridge with its own protocol and hierarchies and punishments for those who do not conform, requiring a finely-judged balancing act at all times.

A girl I knew at university left her course suddenly and took a job as a receptionist with an advertising firm. And as if someone had tripped a switch, everything about her changed at the same time. She had not been prone to laughing at the slightest provocation before. Suddenly, without warning, everything we talked about tended to produce small kitten sounds of amusement in her, or expressions of child-like surprise – mostly a giggle, quickly suppressed by a hand half-covering the mouth. Then too, there was the developing slight stoop to her shoulders, as though she were trying to reduce her height in order to look up into faces instead of at them. It all seemed to happen overnight. Did she just wake up one morning and decide that the quickest path between two points in her life was a straight line of conformity? I wondered how she would feel about that in ten years' time. Perhaps it surprised me more because she had always seemed immune to the traditional pressures to be compliant and non-assertive.

It's supposed to be one of the freedoms a city offers: release from the crippling effects of a single controlling peer group, unified in its attitudes and prejudices. Perhaps outside the boundaries of any significantly sized city, anywhere in the world, there is a more than even chance of a sudden closing of ranks, a mental set that stares back at you from a veranda, from behind a counter, with one unblinking cyclopean eye that will never allow you to forget your otherness.

The light harsh on my eyelids.

It's the hospital evenings I dislike the most. The light like a solid object, pressing down, trying to break into my shadowed world like a lobbed stone entering cool green water.

The murmur of visitors. The faster whisper of nurses' shoes, a slight squeak on the polished floors as they turn corners, checking watches, thinking dressings, medications, reports. A lingering sense of tea-urns, and later, in the darkness, the awareness of ageing flowers. No, it's the leaves you smell first, starting their slow decay in still water. I can hear the vases being put into the corridor for the night, a dull ceramic clink, like bricks being stacked. Strangely, that is when I sense the flowers are most pungent, when they've just been removed.

Deeper into the darkness sedation wears off. That's when you start to hear pain.

It was considered a serious breach of etiquette to make any noise in my uncle's house, but particularly while he was trying to sleep. He was especially irritable the next day if the door had been rattled by the wind the night before, or even if the occasional dog had barked. Not that many did. Although there is obviously more choice about pets in the suburbs than in the centre of Tokyo, the area where we lived was still curiously lacking in animal life. Even birds were not common. When someone walked a dog people stopped in their tracks and stared until it was almost out of sight. There was an added dimension to the curiosity of this event in the heart of the city: imagine the luxury implied by the ownership of a pet as big as a dog – the size of the apartment for a start.

For my sixth birthday, my father had bought me two goldfish called Bashō and Buson, who immediately took control of a large bowl lined with pebbles and rocks and spent their days alternating between a tiny grove of waving greenery and a small blue and gold pagoda. We decided that they obviously left the confines of the bowl at night and flew back to the moon (their natural habitat) from where they decided which part of the world they would explore while we slept. 'Global fish, definitely,' my father solemnly agreed, 'and the world is their oyster!' We sent them on bizarre adventures everywhere: from supermarkets in New York's Chinatown to rivers winding through the Amazon, and then for good measure to a desert or two. They battled through unlikely sequels to most of the films and books that came our way and performed brilliantly for a while as Tintin-style reporters for *The Fishy Times*, a hand-written newspaper with collaged pictures that was destined never to be as widely read as it deserved. As a Christmas present for my parents I devised a puppet play for Bashō and Buson and recreated them for the event from two orange socks with diamond button eyes. The scenery kept collapsing and the music grew increasingly irrelevant to the plot, but the audience seemed to love it just the same. When my mother and I left America I kept the socks but reluctantly transferred ownership of my fish to a painter friend of my parents, who understood their complicated history and said he thought he could provide an environment where they would thrive. I have to admit that the last time I saw them, gleaming in the morning light, their bowl absorbing the deep green of a patterned cloth beneath it, they seemed happy enough.

I wondered if my uncle would mind goldfish, who were silent, after all. Then I thought, perhaps given the choice, he would prefer them to me. I dreamed of the complex and wonderful ways in which I would one day make my escape. Meanwhile, as I became an expert on the nature of silences, I discovered that they were rarely complete. I found the thousand small sounds in day-silences and the breath rhythms and timber creaks of night-silences; not to mention the endless variations in between, involving doors and taps and fans and clocks and paper and insects.

There were nights when my mother took two packets of her sedative instead of one and fell into a deep sleep zone that gave her face a mask-like quality as though she had left her body and slipped outside to briefly known freedom again. At times such as these I had a tendency to wake quickly in the night, my heart hammering against my ribs as I peered through the gloom at her futon, willing her to stir or breathe deeply, anything to disturb the white stillness of her face. The next morning as she moved quietly about the room, I could not speak to her about any of this. If she was becoming even more introspective and reserved, then so was I.

At some point it occurred to me that whilst I had many fears, including the nameless anxieties about my mother's state of mind, so too must my uncle have been afraid – in his case of the loss of absolute control he had once exerted over his sister. Her lethargy alternately perplexed and angered him, but also removed her in some definitive way from the small world where his word was law. One day, out of the blue, he announced that we would be taking a trip to Kyoto to see the autumn leaves, that we would be staying at a hotel overlooking Nijo Castle, and that I would finally appreciate what it was to be a daughter of Japan. The idea of escaping our house for a while thrilled me, as did the expected trip on the bullet train. When the day of the journey arrived I decided to make sure I would not fail to record a single detail. I secreted pieces of paper about my person, in pockets, in folded-back cuffs, in packets of tissues, so that I could record my observations whenever I was left alone. The inevitable result was that my slips of paper escaped at the most inconvenient times, fluttering into the carriage under the gaze of startled businessmen, like irreverent bird-messengers of release.

Kyoto, far less hectic than central Tokyo, was initially disappointing in its apparently similar combination of greyness and neon and bus fumes. But the hotel room had a magic window that looked out over Nijo Castle, all the way to the famous mountains that lay just beyond the city, and for long moments I was transported into the past with an excitement that had the same effect on me as hope. My mother too seemed in better spirits since our arrival. Although she had taken to wearing a darker version of western clothes since coming back to Japan, she allowed me to choose for her two new cheerful cotton *yukatas* for home wear, one covered with bamboo shoots, the other with fans and flowers. For me there was a fabric cat, cut somewhat crazily in one haphazard hit out of a piece of printed fabric and then padded and sewn on to a cushion. It struck me (in a way that I felt rather than understood) as a symbol of both old and new: the traditional good luck emblem one sees everywhere – the cat with one paw raised – usually in 'cute' ceramic form, but this time emerging triumphant out of a spontaneous gesture to present-day creativity and so, for me, also representing the good luck that you can shape for yourself.

Even my uncle seemed less severe when we arrived at the gardens of the Imperial Palace for 'Autumn Leaf Viewing'. It was an extraordinary sight. First the merged colours smudged in like pastel in the distance, and then later the shock of standing beneath an individual tree and looking up into a sky blazing with red and gold light. Relaxed groups of visitors strolled along the paths, admiring the classical architecture, the graceful curve of a roof here, the grandeur of a gate there. At some stage we came to an isolated pond crossed by a slender bridge and there, perched on a rock not far from where we paused, a crane. He was so still that at first he was indistinguishable from the background. But then his head moved a fraction and sunlight flashed across an eye and he emerged as though a lens had drawn him abruptly into focus. What gave him that sense of pride, so obvious in the way he held his head? Was it the same knowledge that allowed him the confidence of stillness? I watched him survey the pond and then the sky, saw the rightness of him in his domain. The weather changed quickly on that day, as it often does in autumn, and a few leaves were falling as we made our way back to the gate. The chill in the air seemed to take some of the joy out of the visit and I wondered whether we would ever again know the same respite, the brief pretence that our sad little household was some sort of family.

Throughout Japan the first cold snap is usually enough to send images not of winter but of the following spring into our minds, into store windows and magazines and temple festivals and classrooms. We can't wait for it to happen again, this brief perfection of living things that permeates even our practical unlovely cities. Our religions (wisely) have drawn it into their rituals, of which there are many. These days there is an abundance of beliefs, all overlapping and intertwined – religions, traditions, superstitions, mythologies – categories enough to cover any need, any eventuality: Shinto for weddings, Buddhism for funerals; lucky and unlucky everything – days, directions, colours, numbers, flowers; ways to improve your chances of good marks, wealth, success in marriage, healthy children, long life, relief from rheumatism. We try, with our various small distractions, to ignore the endless winter. Yet again we are mildly astonished at our reserves of patience – other people's, that is. Inside, each of us is pacing, a restless tiger in a chilly papered cage, aware of the passing of another tiger-taming year. The need for one, just one beautiful thing, to see us through. The way our eyes linger on the meticulously displayed produce in the food sections of department stores. The colours of beans and peppers and mushrooms – the colours of life. What has been drained from our winter faces and clothes resurfaces as splintered neon, flashing back at us from shiny pavements and roads. Salarymen in long raincoats and office girls in thick scarves and tiny skirts push heedlessly past each other, shop-lit mannequins wandering through the biggest perpetual-motion toy-shop in the world.

❧

On our return from Kyoto everything slipped back into the usual pattern. My lessons too continued as before with my tutors seemingly as much afraid as I was of breaking the austerity of silence that hung over our house. It was as though the dark corners of the rooms passed judgement, not only on light but on all forms of sound as well. Music would have seemed like sacrilege.

Calligraphy was another matter. It flowed quietly. Sometimes in fine weather my tutor and I would even take my low writing table outside and I would lose myself in the forming of characters on a page, while the sun warmed the little pool of ink beside me to a gentle pungency. My mother had begun teaching me how to write ideograms while we were still living in America. 'And what I'm showing you now was first imagined in China nearly four thousand years ago,' she said softly one day as she helped me to make firstly the symbol for tree and then, by adding roots at the bottom and simplifying it still further, to draw the character for 'origin'. When we put 'origin' and 'sun' together and made the word for Japan (which all Japanese children know means 'origin-of-the-sun')

she told me the story of Amaterasu Omikami, the deity
who is said to have given birth to the Japanese people.

In the beginning the great Sun Goddess, Amaterasu
Omikami, had decreed that the Land-of-Reed-Plains
(as Japan was known to the Gods) be the place where
her descendants would settle and flourish, which they
did. She even sent her grandson down to earth with
the sacred mirror, sword and jewels that were to
become Japan's Imperial treasures. The brother of the
Goddess was the restless provoker of storms, Susanoo,
who loved nothing better than showing off his
strength. On a day when the heavens were very quiet
and there was no one else about, Susanoo decided to
create havoc, just for the sake of proving his power. He
blew and blew until he had made a monstrous wind
that destroyed Amaterasu's masterpiece, a magnificent
heavenly garden. The Sun Goddess was too shocked
and deeply saddened by this pointless destruction to
do anything but retire to the darkness of a cave behind
a heavy door of rock. In this way the world came to be
plunged into darkness, and its inhabitants became cold
and ill with despair. Then a young female deity did the
only thing she could think of to restore a little joy: she
began dancing. Soon musicians joined in to accompany her and those around gradually began to laugh
and sing and briefly to forget the troubles that had
beset them. Amaterasu was intrigued by the music and
the laughter she heard and couldn't resist peering
outside to see what was happening. As soon as the
strongest deity saw a chink of light appear from behind

the rock door he pulled on it with all his might and Amaterasu came shimmering before her people once more and her light and warmth enabled life to flourish in the world again.

My mother knew many stories and began telling them to me as soon as I could understand words so that it soon seemed I had been born knowing such things. One night in July she told me about Tanabata, the festival celebrating the love of two celestial beings, a weaver and a herdsman, which resulted in them both neglecting their heavenly duties to the fury of the Heavenly Emperor. As punishment he placed the lovers, in the form of two stars, on opposite sides of the Milky Way, permitting them to meet only once a year, on the seventh night of the seventh month, when a bridge would be formed between them by the wings of a company of heavenly magpies. This bridge would only be formed, however, if it was a clear night. If it rained the lovers would have to wait until the next year.

'What date is it?' I asked anxiously.

'Only the fifth,' she replied, 'and it's not really raining, just spitting. There's still time for it to clear.'

And so we stood there, looking up into the twentieth-century American sky, checking the weather on behalf of two unlucky lovers from the dawn of Japanese mythology.

My calligraphy teacher in Japan, Mr Tomo, was as thin as a whisper of brush-writing himself, an uncoiled letter in an ancient black suit that might well have been his father's. I had the feeling he lived on nothing but cup noodles and the sort of take-away *bento* boxes that kept most of Tokyo half-alive throughout the working week. His bony finger would slowly trace a letter and then suddenly flick upwards or downwards like an insect skimming a pond, to show me a preferred variation on what I had just painted, and I would come back with a small surprise from whatever reverie had been claiming me. Back to the present and the all-important page with its indelible record of my progress, or lack of it. We were both aware that my uncle always inspected the results.

The stories behind the characters were probably what fascinated me most at that time. The idea that the drawing for ten thousand began with an image representing ten thousand gods, the character for hair was based on a mandarin's beard, two moons rising behind two mountains was 'many', an arrow in the chest represented a doctor, a man standing by his horse meant 'mail', a knife paring flesh from bone had become 'to separate', and the combined symbols for 'temple' and 'say' together made 'poetry'. At night the characters all had walk-on parts in my dreams, clothed in fabulous costumes, roaming through castles and clouds like ancient sorcerers with fantastic powers.

I became fascinated too at how much the country was still so immersed in the past where its written language was concerned. Learning to write was like taking a stroll through Japanese history, getting regular close-ups of earlier domestic life. Rice, for example, was everywhere: vapour rising from it made 'spirit' or 'energy', fire added to bundled rice stalks represented autumn, stalks and a mouth together meant 'peaceful, happy or harmonious' and one single grain was enough to stand for 'white'.

My mother said it was only after reaching America that she really understood the quiet impact of rice on Japanese daily life, the way it washes our islands like some kind of conceptual white sea. Abroad, she was suddenly aware of its relative absence, the way it no longer accompanied every meal – the white vehicle, the neutral background against which flavours and textures ran comparative riot. In foreign supermarkets it failed to claim an entire section for itself, along with sake. Growing up in Japan you form the impression that rice has existed in every facet of life, forever. In earlier times we crushed the grain up to make our first face powder, used it as our earliest form of starch for clothing. Even today it remains the precious commodity of religious ceremony, raw or cooked into cakes, arranged on a sheet of white paper to symbolise purity, and placed in the *tokonoma*, the special raised alcove in a Japanese home, as an offering to the God who descends to revitalise the world at New Year. If you want to know about your chances of good fortune in the forthcoming year you must, according to an old tradition, stir the New Year rice with a special split stick to see how many grains adhere to it.

The longer I lived in Japan the more I realised how

much we seemed to need these reminders of our roots in the natural world. Even today, in the glitziest department stores, our most valued ceramics are the ones that open like perfectly imperfect flowers, reveal a glimpse of another world through the sketched dragon-fly's wing or the painted leaf. In mirrored columns you will catch sight of birds hiding wisely in the bottom of bowls, petals dancing on the rim of a cup. In the middle of Tokyo people buy the hand-made, with its echo of everything their lives lack, as a talisman, a reminder of future promise: in the spring they will go to Kudanshita to see the blossom, in autumn to Nara for the leaves, and someday they will get out of the city altogether, and find themselves again.

Why did I go on accepting visitors in the room above the incense shop, so many complex individuals with the hidden need to unburden a life? That is difficult to say. Did I, after the breakdown of my marriage, have the greatest need of all — to fill an unbearable emptiness in my own life? To make an art form out of an avoidance of evenings? Was it the desire to know what really went on behind the blank impassive faces in the street outside? Or was it simply a longing to redress an imbalance of power that had lain like a stone inside me for so long? Perhaps it was all of these things. I believe there were some times when I helped. At others what I encountered was outside my realm altogether.

Mr K. is in the music industry, an executive with a bottomless expense account, a beautiful wife and a large house built by a leading avant-garde architect. You know already when I say these things that something is wrong. Because when it looks this stylish and successful from the outside, something is always wrong. This time it's death. He believes he is going to die. That is to say, not right now, or even next month, but sometime. The doctors can't find anything wrong, but he just knows. Or perhaps it's the unbearable pressure of work and he's quietly going a little mad – in the coolest possible way because he's in the music business – but a little mad all the same.

'I don't know, perhaps the weather . . . this season . . . the humidity. I try to be away if I can, but this year everything's been against me.

'To think of the way I started out, when I first landed up here from Hokkaido. That miserable little hovel I rented. It's what got me started in a way. I only knew one thing, that I had to escape from that crap hole and Make It – have space and air-conditioning and all the rest. And now I've got them but I can still feel the water – I'm sorry – the weather pressing in at the windows. I see the way people look when they arrive for work, half-dead already, and I know I could go under at any time and be right back there with them. Record piracy, downloading from the net – this industry's always waiting for the sword to fall.'

It's quite true that life is hell during the rainy season. All over Tokyo, people in tiny rooms swelter their nights away and then wake to go to offices that are even smaller and stuffier. It is a time for putting anything not in immediate use into tightly-sealed plastic bags with dessicant sachets inside so that your entire life does not go mouldy. A time when trains and buses come alive with the sudden flick and blur of dozens of hand-held fans like coloured moths gasping for air. It is in spring and autumn that we think and create and change our lives. In winter, and in the gagging airlessness of the rainy season, we just try to forget. And yet, even at these times we are eternal good citizens, always prepared. Businessmen in their inevitable suits have the name-brand umbrella, the fan, the small folded towel for dabbing at the forehead during rush-hour, the newspaper folded Japanese-style so that a quarter-page can be read at a time without one taking up more than an implicitly allocated space. Sometimes in the rainy season it is as though everything is in slow-motion, as though you can see people drawing even further into themselves to conserve energy while they wait for the season – and life – to pass. So much of life tied up in waiting, for the train to arrive, the week to finish, the promotion to turn up, and above all for that beautiful temporary relief from humidity, the God-gift – rain.

And so we spoke of the weather at length. Of what it meant to him. Of where he'd lived when he first arrived from his parents' modest home in Hokkaido.

Of how disappointed he'd been ('and, let's be frank, a touch relieved') that they did not want to move away from there and live closer to him in Tokyo when he'd hit the Big Time. How he'd thought, when he was young and had never travelled away from his own region, that snow was the worst thing people could experience; how unprepared he'd been. And then he talked about his first job, the few friends he'd made, a girl he'd known, and again, the pressure of the music industry, the unbelievable pressure to get it together before the competition moved in on the same territory, to get the right girl matched to the right song for the next season but ready to go *this* season (and how the hell did you ever really know who would have The Voice, The Look, The Sound?). All you did know for sure was that in this market she had to be young – always younger, more vulnerable and with bigger eyes and a higher voice than the year before. And then if she was a fantastic success you still had to keep at it, looking for the next one, because the shelf-life was getting shorter too and these days their agents knew about everything, every single loophole, and if a contract wasn't watertight it would be your fault and you could be out on your ear overnight, selling jewellery and fake Buddhas outside a station somewhere and paying protection money to a guy with two missing pinkies.

'What happened to your old friends and the girl you mentioned?'

'Nothing. I moved on. We split up and I never saw her again.'

'And you got on with your life?'

'Yes, I moved on. And then I met my future wife at a concert. Of course I gave my career everything I could but there's no denying it would've taken longer without contacts. But then, the whole of society works that way, It's normal. My wife's father could never deny her anything, even me. And so he helped. I like to think it didn't make so much difference overall.'

'You have children?'

'Yes, a girl and a boy. Both complete deadheads at school. My wife's at her wits' end but what can I do? It's her business really. She's home all day long. Personally I think, "So what?" School's got nothing to do with how I got where I am. That's not what counts today. Perhaps it never was. I suppose I'm just going to do my bit by teaching them to sort out what they want as fast as they can and then go for it. You have to know what you want from the world – and how to take it.'

'You seem to have been very successful at that.'

'Yes. I just wish I could get more sleep. Well, I fall asleep fairly quickly after a couple of night-caps, but then a few hours later I'm wide awake and that's it for the night. I'm prowling the house, making tea, watching travelogues of the scenic highlights of Guam or channel-flipping to some idiot filleting fish. Why is there always someone filleting fish on television at three in the morning?'

'When did it start, the sleeplessness?'

'Just out of the blue. An ordinary week, the usual

round of work with a break or two. I'd taken a couple of hours after lunch one day to do some browsing through a few record stores. Had a coffee, walked back to the office through a park. Spotted an old girlfriend again – not to speak to, at a distance. She was at some sort of temple. It was odd, really. She turned around with her hands together in front of her and just looked at me. It made me feel uneasy, seeing her like that after so long, not really knowing what happened. I'd just left, you see. I'd just left and I never actually knew what happened . . .

'I was quite fond of her, truth to tell. I could've become seriously interested but I had other things to worry about – survival for one. Anyway, the last time I saw her was not something I'm particularly proud of. I was due to go off on a fishing trip that weekend and before I left she just blurted it out, told me she was "late". Talk about shock-horror. I was paralysed with fear. Saw myself back in the middle of nowhere with a tribe of squalling brats to feed. Not what I had in mind at all. She should have taken more care . . . I thought it was better all round if I made a break there and then. I knew what would happen if I tried to discuss it rationally. I can't stand the way women seem to completely lose it at times like these. What practical purpose is there in tears? I can't think of any man I know who doesn't feel like running for the nearest exit if a woman looks as though she's about to start crying. So, in essence, after the trip I . . . didn't see her again. It's absurd that after all this time she's come into my mind so strongly; it's as though she's in there all the time, like a presence . . .'

'You saw her at a temple?'

'Yes, well I thought I did. Later I couldn't be absolutely sure, but it had me worried I suppose because of the location – all those things in the ground – grotesque, somehow.'

'Grotesque?'

'Pinwheel things. Pink pinwheels. I kept going back after that, hoping I'd catch sight of her and that I could tidy up the loose ends, find out what she'd decided to do after I left. But I never saw her again. I decided to use a detective. I wanted it sorted out. All kinds of things were going through my mind, which could have been partly lack of sleep, but still . . . I've got a family, a position; I had to consider all the angles.'

'Yes, of course.'

'I got a preliminary report. The temple was recent and not, strictly speaking, the real thing, but they'd nabbed an opening in a lucrative market. They were charging big money for symbolic offerings and Buddhas to guard aborted foetuses – "water babies". You see what I'm telling you? I realised then that she'd taken the only course of action I would have thought feasible, all those years ago. She'd "made a water baby". I didn't know what the repercussions might be. What did it mean if she still had guilt or grief feelings about an unborn child after this long? I asked the agency to hurry up with tracing her. By now I was becoming very edgy. I'd heard of other pseudo-religious set-ups like this one, extorting huge sums of money from women who had trouble coming to terms with abortion, even intimidating them by putting up warnings of all the shit that could follow if the soul of the unborn was not appeased by pricey memorial services. Not that someone broke and alone has much choice about abortion I suppose; an illegitimate birth on the family register doesn't exactly help if you're looking for work. The full investigation took less time than I thought. It was true that she'd ended the pregnancy and then she just ... died. She'd stopped eating. By the time they got her to hospital it was too late. The thing is that I couldn't have seen her there at the temple. I couldn't have. But now she's got into my head somehow and I can't get her out. I know she's waiting for me – standing among those pinwheels, waiting for me to die ...'

One evening my mother was there, fresh from her bath, wearing the bamboo-patterned robe we had chosen together, and the next morning she was not – only a faint depression in the futon, a curve like a wave in a white sea.

I remember being hurried half-asleep by my uncle into another room before it was light, being wrapped in a quilt and told that it was still very early and that I must on no account make a noise. And then another quilt on top of the first and the heat of them making me thirsty and drowsy all at once so that I fell into a restless dream of deserts where sand blew repeatedly across my mouth to prevent me from crying out.

Later that day I crept back to look at my mother's futon. On the floor by the bed, not one or two empty packets of her sleeping draught, but many. A sense of the fibres of the *tatami* imprinting themselves on the soles of my feet as I stood still, waiting, listening, endlessly looking between the white wave and the white paper packets, becoming colder and colder until the ache in my legs rose to fill my whole body.

My uncle did not admit what had happened for some time. Perhaps he was even trying to deny it to himself. He said my mother had been taken ill and that my seeing her would only make her worse. I think in the end the realisation that she was dead, must have been dead when I first looked down on her empty futon, came to me via a few gentle oblique words from one of my tutors, who did not realise my ignorance of the truth and who mistook my quietness for normal grief. I cannot remember how I finally came to terms with the fact that she would never return. I know that my deepest rejection of my uncle also stemmed from around this time, but oddly I cannot reconstruct this segment of my past. It is as though my mind has closed off a period of terrible darkness and the key is lost.

I can only recall one brief glimmer of light: visiting a park with my calligraphy teacher, Mr Tomo. It was a typical haven for Japan, with several smaller shrines grouped around a larger one. I remember the shape of a huge bell, of thinking that it looked very strong and solid, as though it would last forever, and how surprising that seemed.

And then we were looking down into water and my teacher was pointing and saying, 'Look, do you see it, just behind the rock?'

It was a carp – a sudden exquisite red-gold shimmer against the muddy background. In that moment something strange happened to me. It was as though the sunlight passed right through me to touch the fish and bring the beauty of it to life; as though I, as I had always known myself, had simply ceased to be. I was between the light and the fish and yet a part of them at the same time, and for a second I felt no more sadness, only the warmth of the sun against my coat and the passing back of the colour through my eyes.

When I review the remainder of that time in my uncle's house I find I cannot recall the colour of things there, only a sense of the absence of colour. Even the food, prepared and left ready for us by a practically invisible caterer, seemed pallid and tasteless. I would get up in the morning knowing only that I faced a series of tasks before I would be allowed to rest again. Sometimes, just thinking about all the things necessary to keep a human being alive made me tired. I wanted to be left alone to sleep forever. It was at those times I would try to remember the day at the temple, the fish, and exactly how I had felt as I watched it. It was all I had to hold on to.

Again, it was Mr Tomo who noticed when I had a slight fever and mentioned it to my uncle, who did not seem particularly concerned. His only remark to me later was, 'You have been neglecting your studies for some time now. Let us reapply ourselves to the business of the Living.'

How did the miracle of Mrs Matsu occur? I am somehow aware that she must have arrived in my uncle's house very early on that first day, before I was properly awake. An impression of a hand briefly on my brow, and later, voices raised in another room. I remember being impressed by the firmness of the stranger's tone, a voice – a female voice – for the first time equal in strength, in its own way, to my uncle's. And then we were introduced: a friend of Mr Tomo, a teacher of *sumi-e* – Japanese brush-painting. My surprise at finding the image so different to what I'd imagined from the voice I'd overheard. A figure so modestly and soberly dressed she might have been any suburban housewife on the way to get vegetables for soup at the local market. Neat hair, a sensible (albeit sensitive) face. The sort of woman that a Japanese man longs for – in a wife. The sort you can depend on to have a meal or a bath ready on command, to pack the right number of essentials in a case for a business trip and, later, to be waiting with a sympathetic smile to hear all the news.

But Mrs Matsu was not a housewife. She had been married only briefly many years ago to her lover, a man of whom her parents would inevitably disapprove, a fellow artist whose paintings and woodcuts were later to hang in museums throughout the country, whose heart had never been suspected of having a flaw, and who collapsed in a subway underpass one Friday night, a month after their marriage, the passing commuters thinking him just another salaryman slipping into alcoholic oblivion. After that Mrs Matsu poured her passion even more completely into her work and became a respected artist in her own right, her reputation emerging as a by-product of the path she took, not an end in itself, much as water might influence a landscape on its journey elsewhere.

At different times in her life Mrs Matsu had made study trips abroad and the breadth of her experience made it all the easier for her to understand my multi-layered confusion, although I think she would have known instinctively how to relate to any child; it was in her nature to get to the core of people very quickly.

She began our lessons in the best possible way, by telling me a story. It concerned the last days of a revered artist called Wu Tao-Tzu, who was asked by the Emperor to paint a landscape on one of the walls of the palace. When the work was completed it could be seen that, in the very centre, the artist had included the image of an open cave. The Emperor could not praise the painting highly enough, and while he was still marvelling aloud at the skill of Wu Tao-Tzu's brush, the artist calmly walked up to the mouth of the cave, entered it, and disappeared. Not only did Wu Tao-Tzu disappear, but so too did the entire painting, vanishing from the wall after him.

Brush-painting then, even from the earliest times, was believed to be more than decoration; technique was more than mere cleverness. The acquisition of such a skill was allied from the start with elements of the supernatural, a mastery arising from a lifetime of spiritual and physical training, beginning with the way one seated oneself before the paper, the inhaling and exhaling of breath. Was the story also a reminder of impermanence, the need for non-attachment to what was physically present? I liked the idea of the joke Wu Tao-Tzu had played on the court. I visualised their cold sardonic faces as they observed the modestly-dressed artist performing his painted miracles for their pleasure and then their shocked open mouths as he took his leave. Did he turn to look at them one last time with a gleam in his eye, before disappearing? No, I decided, he would have been above that. He would have been very composed to the end, looking straight ahead, needing to focus completely on where he was headed. And then afterwards chaos would have erupted. Some of the women would have screamed, others fainted. I could see several of the men reaching for their swords, looking to the corners of the room for ghosts, and there would have been those who just stood stock still, their eyes bulging, their faces purple with disbelief. I laughed out loud at the triumph of Wu Tao-Tzu, at the way he had chosen to solve the unsolvable, the terrible mismatch between the perfection he could visualise and the world in which he lived. I laughed more and more, forgetting the censorious house. I laughed until, at last, I cried.

And then I picked up my brush.

I had of course been applying certain basic principles of brushwork to my calligraphy lessons, but I had not painted anything with a real sense of spontaneous joy since leaving America. Now, with the encouragement of Mrs Matsu, I began to look at what was around me and to imagine how I could capture movement, the sense of light on a wing or on water, the suddenness of the wind. Now the formal garden behind my uncle's house was teeming with life: ants and beetles alone produced dynasties, founded empires and fought territorial wars out there and all with a total disregard for the pettiness of human politics. Humans were surely just larger versions of insect life and, it seemed to me then, more capable of gratuitous cruelty to each other than so-called lesser creatures. I decided to focus on nature for a while. I began to paint the first four 'honourable gentlemen' of *sumi-e*: the bamboo representing summer, the chrysanthemum for autumn, the plum blossom of winter and the Chinese orchid, spring. Much later in life I would go into the countryside and find a place by a river where I could paint undisturbed, and there I would wait with the brush before me, unable to paint the fish until I too could feel the water pushing me forward as a leaf is carried by the wind, until I could sense sunlight flash on scales as I curved to avoid a rock, my knowledge of self the only certainty needed.

Various medical staff come at intervals to move my limbs and test for reflexes. A voice speaking louder than usual requesting me to squeeze a hand or open my eyes if I can hear or understand. The voice raised expectantly, authoritatively, in the manner of people who speak to the blind or to someone who cannot understand their language. Afterwards the scratching sound of a pen across paper and the metal 'click' as a clipboard is replaced on the end of the bed. I have been assessed.

One morning after this, a young girl with a rattling tray of cups mistakes me for another patient on her list and tries to lift my head and give me something to drink. I know from the vaguely-sensed tenderness in my arm that I am being fed intravenously. How else would I continue to wait for my body to come to life again? She tries to lift my head and presses a cup to my lips. And there is a cry struggling to my throat, 'You don't understand. I can't drink from a cup. Take it away. Please . . . take it away.' But all that comes out is a wild throat sound as warm liquid washes over my mouth and down into my gown.

By way of my classes with Mrs Matsu, I gradually started to reclaim elements of my personality that until then had been in danger of disappearing. I allowed myself to be curious, not in a hunted furtive way, but in the normal manner of children the world over: I began all over again to enjoy asking questions. Mostly I wanted to know what she had observed about the differences between countries she had visited – how children were raised, how other people lived in places I had only read about, whether she had found the norms confusing in the way I so often did.

'Yes,' she said, smiling at her own memories, 'when I studied here in Japan I was the rebellious student who refused to silently accept the teacher's every direction. Abroad I was seen as "the quiet little Japanese lady" who was relatively self-effacing and polite to a fault. Sometimes people will see in you what they expect to find. You will have to get used to the idea that in the course of your life you may be judged from radically different perspectives, depending on the needs or biases or inadequacies of others. You can learn a great deal about them, just by listening. It is never too early to start practising "detached aware-ness" where opinions are concerned.'

It seemed no time at all passed between the start of my classes with Mrs Matsu and the discussion of plans to send me to a highly-regarded girls' boarding school on the other side of Tokyo. Although I was nervous about being plunged into a totally new world with so little notice to adjust to the idea, another part of me, one that longed for company and friends and new ideas rushed to embrace it. I had no family to regret leaving now, and while I was initially saddened at the thought of not seeing Mr Tomo and Mrs Matsu on such a regular basis, they promised that they would always be there for me and that we could still meet up at weekends and holidays. They had both come to seem far closer and dearer to me in the short time I had known them than my uncle who would surely be as glad as I was at my forthcoming departure from his house.

My school, when I arrived, astonished me. Firstly the student body was representative of almost every country I could think of, so that my first impression was that I'd somehow landed in the middle of New York. And then the pleasure of finding that, apart from reasonable discipline, we were actually encouraged to run around and make a noise on the sports field, to cheer each other on at swimming and gymnastics. And above all, we were allowed to make music. The other girls, at first thinking I was rather stand-offish, soon realised I was just as shy as they were, and it wasn't long before I made friendships that lasted, in many cases, through university and into our globally scattered adult lives.

The only negative memory that I have from this time is of a recurring dream, where I am walking down a street, an ordinary Japanese street with small steam-laden food shops crowded up against over-stocked clothing outlets and vegetable sellers. There is a railway overpass in the distance, and all around me traffic fumes, noise, people. At some point I turn slightly and, out of the corner of my eye, I notice a figure in the background. I walk a little faster, past a coffee shop, a supermarket selling imported foods, a gift shop where a crate of new goods is being unpacked, the china catching the light as it is lifted from the straw. I turn corners, walk for what seems like hours until it is almost dusk and then, as though I cannot help myself, I glance over my shoulder and find with a chill that the same dark shape has been there all along, turning every corner I turn, and no matter how fast I walk it is always there, the same distance behind me. I notice one other thing about this nameless figure: the left shoulder is sloping lower than the right and I feel I should know what this means but, in spite of all my efforts, it still eludes me. I know only that it fills me with a sense of dread and helplessness and that this itself is enough to cause my heart to beat faster and faster until I am forced awake, listening in sudden exhausted relief to birds in the dawn light.

Z. never used his surname. He was the first westerner to ask for my help. Not help so much as an ear, a neutral person who would not have any hidden agenda or want anything from him.

He is not deeply interested in history, in the Heian period or in poetry, but a contact suggested he might find it rewarding to speak to me. He came to Japan straight from a Midwest law course. In a three-piece suit and a stylish raincoat he'd been paying off for a year. By the time he'd been in Tokyo three months he was wearing chains and black leather – outside working hours, that is. He didn't really know how his life had slipped into another gear so quickly. He'd wanted to take some time out, that was all. There was a girl back in Something-or-other-Fields, very loving and considerate with diamond rings in her eyes from the age of seventeen when they'd first started going together. It was just that the stress of needing to succeed at everything, the parental expectations, the study fighting the part-time work, the repeated gearing up to, and then the postponing of, the engagement . . . By the time he'd finished his course he felt like a middle-aged man who'd lost sight of everything that once used to matter. And he hadn't done any Living, not to speak of. He could see the life he was supposed to follow all around him, the various stages illustrated by people he knew, like highlighted signs on a road map. Others were doing it over and over for him. The same life. Over and over. How many of those lives would be chosen again, if the protagonists had a choice, he wondered. Were even their limited satisfactions genuine, or was it all a no-going-back-now rationalisation? Could anyone ever tell the difference? He'd thought a little distance might help. God, the tears they'd shed. Anyone would have thought he'd been going off to war. When he got off the train at Tokyo station he thought he had. Two days later he answered an ad in an English-language magazine for an apartment share: two Japanese guys and a fellow American. Happy to have someone new to the city, interested in helping him make social contact. A very cool scene. There seemed to be nothing they wouldn't try once, and in Tokyo, that meant a lot. The clubs alone were unbelievable – what was on offer, what was here ('if *only* you'd been here last week . . .'). Anything at all could be bought. Anything. Now he's mentally trying to backtrack, to work out when the taste for novelty turned into an addiction. At some point he began to feel that his head was moving faster than his body ever could, and that the strain was starting to pull him apart. And there were people who turned up at all hours of the day and night, something they thought he might like to try, someone they wanted him to meet. He's been slotted: the perfect customer waiting for the absolute product. One Sunday morning he woke up in a strange bed covered in crumpled lizard print and slid the door back to find an apartment crawling with snakes. Then a man and woman turned up with a bag of warm brioche and asked him if he'd like to get it together again sometime and meet a few of their friends. He didn't even stop to find his shirt. Now the words, 'Hey, man, didn't I see you the other night . . .' have begun to send a shiver down his spine. He's just not remembering stuff any more. Short-term memory loss. Maybe it's just the mobile phone. It rings all the time. 'Hello, hello –

moshi, moshi?' and then usually a laugh. Earlier on he could tell from the laugh if it was sex or drugs or something else, but now all the laughter sounds the same and it's started to have an echo. Although maybe that's the mobile phone too.

He's got all the signs of someone who's gone down with an illness because he never had time to build up antibodies. His hands tremble a lot. He thinks they've noticed at work and it's getting him the wrong kind of attention. The point is, where does he go from here? Not back to Something-or-other-Fields, that's for sure. That's the only thing he does know. Although that girl was nice. She's becoming more and more like someone he saw in an old movie once, a long time ago. You don't meet people like that very often in real life. Most people are too screwed up, want to bleed you dry. You just have to see one of them slide out from a crowd like a pickpocket on the make, come toward you with a hand extended, to know that somebody wants something – again. If only they wouldn't touch him. He can't stand the way complete strangers pat his wrist, put an arm around his shoulder or neck. It makes his skin crawl. If only they'd leave him alone. He can almost imagine going cold turkey and just walking away from the lot. There is the slight problem of finances, of course. Living on the edge has turned out to be frighteningly expensive, even with four sharing. He doesn't know where the others get their money but they sure as hell don't go out to work. Maybe there are some things it's better not to know. Although if he loses his job, he'll need to check out what other people do to keep going. There are plenty of ads but he'd have to get himself in better shape than he is now. Maybe some vitamins. He gets tired so easily these days . . .

'What I think I'd like most right now, this minute, is a place I heard about, in the mountains somewhere, an inn where you can forget everything, where you are looked after completely – a bath prepared when you arrive, a fresh cotton robe, the food brought to you very quietly on a tray, and then the bedding laid out. And in the morning, no noise except for the birds outside. You can lie there and listen to the birds and think of nothing at all. And the wonderful part of it is that no two songs are ever exactly alike. There's something miraculous in that. Human voices have started running into each other for me. You know what I mean? I can't tell one from the other any more. I think that's a bad sign, don't you? But if I could just lie down quietly and listen to those birds for as long as I needed, I think I would be able to sort myself out, and then I'd know what to do next. I'm almost sure of it . . .'

I was still considering my own career options when I was informed that I had reached the age when that small family business was to pass to me – the incense shop in the little street leading off Omotosando. As businesses go, it was modest by today's standards and evidently not worthy of my uncle's time or attention, or I was sure he would have fought to keep control of it himself. In any case he was more than fully occupied with the expansion of his own antiques business, and his letter to me, detailing my inheritance, was cordial.

Kodo. The Way of Incense. A reconsideration of the boundaries of my existence. A reminder of my mother's stories. A continuation of history – our history, that could not be tampered with.

And so I began to alternate between two worlds – my life as a university student and the quiet subtlety of the realm of incense. The battle to attend university had been ongoing ever since it was first proposed to my uncle at a 'Parents' Day' two years before I completed my boarding school education. Afterwards he accompanied me on a tour of the school, his irritability at not being able to smoke evident in every word.

'You are developing regrettable tendencies. You should be focusing on cultivating *onna rashisa*.' By this he meant the Japanese version of femininity which covered everything from polite submissiveness to graceful movement. His hand like a steel trap on my arm. 'You have to work harder than most. Remember you are only half-Japanese.'

His words still had the power to wound. It was as though in the long absences between seeing him for the occasional outing or afternoon tea, I would forget how bad the past had been; I would still be hoping for some token of approval from him. I had no idea what he imagined my future would be, but obviously the scenario did not involve further education along lines of my own choosing. A secretarial course was half-heartedly suggested as he toyed with an unlit cigarette. Flower arranging. Perhaps I simply should have been grateful for the concessions I had already won in childhood with the help of Mrs Matsu. The right not to be further indoctrinated in the ways of the sword; the right to grow up amongst my peers. But by my senior years at school I had been encouraged to think about choices on my own behalf and I had also been able to spend my holidays with friends or with Mrs Matsu, so my uncle's capacity to undermine me at a practical level had waned considerably. I had pushed the cold house with its smothered memories to the farthest corner of my mind, an ink-wash of oblivion, like watery clouds masking a darker sky.

In retrospect I don't know how much I really wanted to go straight from school to university. In one sense I could see it was a continuation of the 'blotting paper' process – the relentless soaking-up of knowledge without yet having tested what I might be capable of doing with it. So many confusions in my mind. The idea that a choice made could not be unmade and that I could be defining everything about my future life on a whim . . . The concept of 'half-Japanese' continued to haunt me as I discovered books about the Second World War period, lent to me by foreign school friends returning from abroad – a different view of history from that portrayed in Japanese texts. Only the dead were the same and yet, even then, their numbers could be denied or magnified, if it could serve a political point or two.

My parents by then were like a distant memory, two people who had once briefly laughed together, given each other time and space and tenderness and love. Their view of life had expanded to embrace the world; my uncle's reduced everything by cutting it down into small elements he could control. Why was he the one allowed to go on? I lived through my teenage years with a hidden yet ongoing sense of precariousness, an unwillingness to become too involved with others. It seemed best. To avoid pain, it seemed best.

Inevitably I spoke of my career options with Mrs Matsu. Imperceptibly she broadened the scope of our discussion to include much that at the time I thought maddeningly irrelevant but that later seemed to hint at who I already was and wanted to be, as much as what I wanted to do.

At some point before I left one day she asked me suddenly, 'Are you still having the dream?' The shadow-figure flashed into my mind. The shoulders. One higher than the other. 'Not so often now,' I said. 'Sometimes.' She looked out of the window, troubled, and put a hand on my arm. I didn't want to dwell on it.

On the basis that I never had enough time to read, no matter how many things I gave up, and because I knew it would have pleased my father, I had decided to study literature at university. And so, like the girl in the fairytale, set to spin straw into gold, my chosen materials multiplied with every passing day, my piles of books grew into a room of books and I lived, palely and vicariously, through the travels and exploits of others, until I was dragged back by exasperated friends into what passed for reality. An occasional life.

Mrs Hana, of whom my mother had briefly spoken when we first returned to Japan, had been managing *The Bridge of Dreams* incense shop for as long as she could remember. She assured me over and over that she was looking forward more than anything to passing the reins to someone else, describing at length how she wanted to spend time embroidering, travelling, seeing more of her grandchildren. And then she picked up a beautiful little ceramic bridge brush-rest that she had been using as a paperweight, and burst into tears. It seemed that the shop was such an integral part of her existence that she could not visualise what her life would be without it. We talked, we drank tea, we decided on a compromise. She would continue as she had always done, taking care of the customers and the store front, and I would stay behind the scenes, an invisible pair of hands dealing with the ordering and the paperwork. We smiled shyly at each other when these details had been worked out. I think we never again had such an intimate conversation, but a warm and quiet understanding seemed to have been established between us that day, and it was as good a basis for a working relationship as any I could have imagined.

We followed our agreement with a slow walk around the store: the polished glass counters; the joss stick holders, some no bigger than a coin, painted with cranes or pine branches; the small ceramic boxes for holding blended incense balls, made in traditional blue-and-white or cast, more exotically, in the form of mythical birds or animals; a selection of burners; some samples of precious woods; a bowl of tiny jewel-bright bags containing fragrant mixtures. Pride of place in an alcove near the back was given to a gold lacquered rack on which garments were once spread for scenting. Beneath the robe a censer containing incense balls would allow fragrance slowly to penetrate every part of a garment. In *The Tale of Genji* mention is made of small censers that were devised to be held briefly inside each sleeve to emphasise the effect of the fragrance, much as today one would apply a dab of perfume to each wrist.

There were two floors above the shop that could also be accessed by a back entrance: an apartment at the top that had recently been vacated by a tenant on her marriage, and a single empty room on the middle level where I stood for some time alone, wondering at the sense of peace and calm it gave me. It dawned on me suddenly that, in Tokyo terms, I had been granted a rare gift – I had inherited space. I could not have foreseen then how life would flow in to fill it.

I remember going, with some university friends, to an exhibition of cloud paintings at a Tokyo gallery and being slightly surprised that so many of the exhibits had already sold. The owner of the gallery shrugged and smiled, 'People are buying a piece of sky, you see. They are prepared to pay for that.' Unarguable. In Tokyo there is no sky. We do not look up. Nor can we often look out. And in order not to go crazy observing the mass of humanity that surrounds us, we simply choose not to see it. People in Tokyo barge straight into others who cross their paths because they have already excluded the possibility of so many potential obstacles coming at them in a single day. This perverse optimism is how they get up in the mornings and face the thought of going through it all over again. And this need for re-framing extends itself to all the other problems of inner-city life that have to be mentally shifted into a more acceptable light. If your apartment is in a shabby building on an ugly street you will absorb nothing of what is before your eyes until you can remove your outdoor shoes and can tend the plants you have on the balcony, or until you can unroll and admire the new futon cover you bought last week. Thus the release we continue to seek through shopping, the national drug.

We dress to go out shopping as we would prepare ourselves for an important date. The bright lights of department stores fill us with open-mouthed delight: the clothing, the jewellery, the DIY sections, the *Hello Kitty* corner with its endless range of personal and domestic 'must-have's including a toaster that even imprints the adored *Kitty* face on a piece of toast as it cooks. And then the electronics floor with its home entertainment systems, its incredible shrinking televisions and videos and sound systems, its games and movies. So many ways to fill up our minds. Even though we know we are victims, most of us go willingly to the slaughter of our weekly budgets at the slightest excuse. To be fully occupied visually, anaesthetised mentally, relieves stress. That is why we go through what we do at work, week after week – to be able to afford this glorious binge of stress release. It doesn't bear thinking about, and so we don't, much. The fact that we are all there together, doing our shopping almost as one unified whole, is in its own way reassuring. The fact that we return week after week as a group is reassuring too, to the department stores themselves, who are acutely sensitive to the slightest fluctuations in our numbers. It is like a long ongoing love affair with its temptations, flirtations, seductions, uncertainties, rejections, and renewals of passion. The image most fondly embraced by the stores is one of faithful coupling: the idea of going hand-in-hand with them into the future, confident lovers in a voluntary bondage of mutual trust. We are the ones with the real power, they tell us in so many ways. If we are just a little more giving they will promise never to tire of anticipating our deepest desires, of amusing us with the absolute latest, of fulfilling our greatest fantasies about ourselves. With love like that an offer, what can we do?

Tokyo galleries are full of western-style art. The city is said to be one of the most exciting in the world in which to be making and exhibiting work these days. As in New York, the sheer number of people generates a peculiar energy which is transformed, in spite of (or because of) the pollution, expense, deprivations and excesses, into contemporary art. And that is the antithesis of everything that is known and respected in brush-painting: sun beating on a plate-glass window versus light filtered through the paper of a *shoji* screen. And the seductions and weaknesses of the invader are, it seems, tied together in the one package. Colour, as much and as quick as you like – mix it up, put it down in great fighting slabs as thick as you like, carve it up, wear it out, eat it if you like. Just do it now and do it big. How will the delicate nuances of ink compete with that? Think of the mental shift required to move from an average dose of colour television, a standard billboard, a street of neon lights, to the white page, the inkstone, the brush in its bamboo holder. For those who still want what ink and brush can provide, the shift, however great, equates with a journey to an oasis.

Mr Q. asks me if I have any calligraphy books from my early school days and so I find what I can and leave them out for him to look at before I join him for our meetings. He speaks to me gently as though to his own daughter:

'I would like you to tell me a different story each week. I want to know if you remember what I used to read to you when you were very tiny. I can still see that very square fringe and your eyes so huge beneath, never blinking as I read to you. And those two red patches on your cheeks in winter, as bright as the mittens I gave you for your fifth birthday. Do you remember going to the Nezu Shrine gardens that day – the way you laughed at the two sculpted frogs sitting on rocks, looking across the water at each other as though they were having a long and interesting conversation? How it seemed we had entered another part of the world there, with the old-style tea-houses – everything wood and bamboo, even the fences made from bamboo bound with twine, and the paths so steep you thought sometimes we were going up a mountain? And all the stone images of Buddha, so many Bodhisattvas and Kannons that it seemed we would be protected for all eternity. Then, by the time you were seven, you could recite all the stories back to me, word perfect, and you had become fascinated by the idea of becoming a young lady and wearing make-up and perfume and having your photo taken wearing your best kimono when you were twenty for "Coming-of-Age" Day, and how you had to make all of that fit in with planning to be a deep-sea diver or a mountain climber.

'When I went away on business trips I would bring back charms from foreign countries, to protect you in case our own gods ever turned their heads for a moment and forgot to be vigilant. I became less convinced of our own national certainties when I started to travel; that is to say, abroad, I found I became instantly more Japanese, more defensive of everything from cooking to temple amulets, but also more troubled. Because *they* were sure of their rightness too, terribly sure in stone and glass and steel. Different gods, the same history of crimes committed in their names. I have yet to draw all these threads together and make a whole of it that I can live with. Once the door has been opened then the concessions, the compromises, are ongoing. I cannot return to my small safe world where you and your mother were my centre and the reason for everything.

'Now I wish to hear again the tale of the bamboo cutter, as closely as you can remember my version of it, told to you so many years ago.'

And so I recreated for him one of the earliest Japanese stories, usually known as *The Bamboo Cutter's Daughter*.

'Once, in ancient times, there lived an old bamboo cutter and his wife, who had never been blessed with any children. One day in the course of his work, the bamboo cutter came upon a bamboo stalk that gave off a marvellous light. Intrigued, he investigated further and discovered, sitting in the hollow of the stalk, a tiny baby. In addition to this miracle he found, in other parts of the same plant, all the gold he would ever need for a long and comfortable life. The bamboo cutter and his wife loved this child completely at first sight and gave due thanks to the gods for such a longed-for event. She was to bring them great joy. With time the little girl grew to be a beautiful woman and inevitably had a large number of suitors, among them many noblemen. Even the sovereign himself fell in love with her. The girl's father, wanting to see her happily married, told her it was now time for her to choose a husband. It was then that she finally felt compelled to reveal her secret. She told her father that no matter how happy and loved she had been as a child, no matter how many suitors would wait for her hand, and no matter how much she wanted to remain on earth, she was – and always had been – a daughter of the moon, and would have to return there before she lived out a normal span of years. The bamboo cutter remembered the soft golden light that had surrounded the bamboo stalk on the day he had found her, and realised that he must always have known, in his heart, that such happiness was only to be granted him for a certain time. He knew too that given the choice, he would accept the terms of his blessing over again without question. The suitors who refused to be turned away and tried to prove their worth by achieving impossible goals all failed terribly or in some cases even died, not for want of courage, but because they had tried to ignore the rulings of destiny. The sovereign was so distraught on discovering the bamboo cutter's daughter had been reclaimed by the moon that he set fire to all her earthly keepsakes, thus producing the smoke that has come from Mount Fuji ever since. And this is how the fragile link she created between earth and sky continues to this day.'

This is all I can do. Repeat the stories for him. Allow him to correct me on certain details from time to time, as gently as though he were talking to a child, as indeed he is. I cannot do anything to change the fact that his daughter died of leukaemia when she was eight. Or that his wife also died some years later. He would have liked to have kept a memento of his daughter, some of her books or drawings perhaps, but a well-meaning relative accidentally disposed of them in a draconian act of housekeeping one day during his absence. Now he brushes a hand over my early attempts at calligraphy, and speaks to me of improvements that will come with time, if I am careful and work at it.

Bizarrely, it was via my uncle that I was introduced to my future husband, at the time a newly employed assistant in my uncle's antiques business. I say 'bizarrely' now because I still cannot believe the extent of my naïveté in believing I had chosen my own fate. My uncle was a supremely detached and astute dealer in precious merchandise and I later came to realise that the ease with which my husband found employment had as much to do with his social connections as it did with any personal or professional abilities. But it was my uncle who knew how to sell, and that is why he owned the business. If he had something he particularly wanted to market he would place it near similar objects that had been left a little dusty or unpolished. He would make sure the light fell on the chosen piece just so, and that all the textures in close proximity to it were somehow special, as though it had the capacity to cast a glow around itself. And the other works placed to the side – at just the right distance to the side – would begin to seem like pale and less interesting imitations, inferior companions to that which had its own special aura. I believe that the two greatest loves of my uncle's life were forged metal and marketing, as effective a two-edged sword as any perhaps, for carving a path through life as he saw it.

My parents conducted their own early romance in a university library. 'A chance meeting, of course!' my father would say with a wicked gleam in his eye when he told the tale. An early photograph shows my mother standing next to him shortly after they were married, his arm around her shoulder, her head leaning back, eyes gazing up into his face. When I first saw it I thought he was demonstrating a classic male posture – the desire to shield his mate from the world – but later, as I looked more closely into their faces, I saw that his was the more vulnerable, and that her look, far from expressing helplessness and potential dependency, was more like that of a mother cat protectively watchful of a bold young kitten who has not yet been bitten by the nettle or the rat.

The only photograph I have of my husband and myself, snapped by a passer-by early in our honeymoon, was meant to be taken overlooking the sea, but he saw something in a window before we crossed the road, and wanted both things – the sweater and the photograph (developed that afternoon so he could send a copy straight off to his mother). And so we do not have the sea behind us, but a plate-glass window. I am searching vaguely across the road in the direction of the waves (looking, as a friend later remarked, as though I might possibly prefer to be under them) and my husband is glancing surreptitiously at the window. Not only at the sweater, but also at his own reflection, checking it for newly acquired imperfections.

What I particularly remember about our own courtship is that, for one reason or another, we were never very much alone. I saw just enough of this man to make me curious, and then to interest me, but the person I grew to love, I later realised, existed largely in my mind. So terribly easy for it to happen. And all the usual suspects – songs, films, even the seasons – doing their bit to convince you that you have a right to this happiness; perhaps that it really is predestined. Later my eyes seemed to see through everyone, sized up every angle, as though I were a camera tracking plot moves. If I had once been cautious, I had by that stage moved a step further; I no longer felt safe in any but the most clearly defined situations, preferably those where I could exercise that ultimate gesture of control – escape at will.

My uncle took it upon himself to accompany us in the early days of outings to parks or festivals or semi-formal meals, a custom I found quaintly archaic. But then, I reasoned, how much harm could this really do, to preserve peace by giving him some illusion of parental authority? He must care something for me, I thought, if he is prepared to go to so much trouble over this. Meanwhile, the man who had been so carefully groomed for me continued to grow in my estimation. He seemed a little reserved to begin with, although charmingly considerate, and interested in my opinions on almost everything. I was astonished at how well his thoughts echoed mine and how quickly we progressed, as if with no effort on our part, to considering ourselves a couple, capable of bursting into spontaneous laughter at the idiocy of the world around us, and rejoicing in our own youth and certainty, in the infinite choices we saw ahead of us. I thought later that it was while we were viewing the blossom together, on the lake at Kudanshita, that I must have first felt I was in love with him, watching a few petals land on his hair and feeling them touch my own. That too was the first time I allowed myself to think of building a future with someone, and of imagining the sort of family closeness I had not known for years.

I was my uncle's only relative. Why had I not seen what an attractive inducement that must have been? While it is customary in Japan, as generally in the west, for a wife to take her husband's surname on marriage, it is also possible – although less common – for the husband to take his wife's name and become one of the small group of *mukoyoshi*, 'adopted sons-in-law'. Such a gesture is not made lightly on either side. It typically happens if a family has no sons and there are substantial business assets to be managed and eventually inherited. Even my socialite mother-in-law was won over by the prospect of the wealth involved in her son 'changing families'.

On our wedding day my husband, very solemn and self-contained, spent more time with my uncle than he did with me. I comforted myself with the thought that he was taking his new responsibilities seriously and that there was, after all, a lifetime for us to spend together in any way we chose. The wedding, however, had changed something between us. He was no longer the laughing considerate companion of our courtship days, but a stern, even rather disdainful, figure who expected to receive, but not necessarily to give. When I said, only half-jokingly, that I hoped he was not going to turn into one of those typical Japanese husbands who were the despair of contemporary women, he turned to me with a look of undisguised anger on his face. 'Obviously the necessary adjustments will take you longer. I had hoped your earlier days in your uncle's house would have made all the difference, but of course the damage had already been done by the time you got there. Believe me, it was a factor that caused me many a sleepless night – your mixed parentage. If it had not been for your uncle's reassurances . . .'

Over the weeks that followed, a paper-thin wall of contempt developed between us that saw us avoiding rather than seeking each other's company. I discovered things about him I could never have guessed from the time we'd spent together. His passion for collecting miniature furry animals in lurid colours, for one. I would wake in the night sometimes to find them staring manically back at me from a shelf, as though waiting for permission from a full moon to spring into violent and destructive life. I found too that he would have preferred me to wear short pleated skirts instead of jeans. 'Look, something like this,' he would explain, leaping up to search through his collection of video-clips of teenage song-and-dance performers until he found the perfect example. 'Now, that's cute,' he'd announce, satisfied that he'd delivered the ultimate accolade. 'But I don't want to look "cute",' I would inevitably reply, feeling that I was stating the obvious. He could only stare back at me, incredulous.

His favourite relaxation at home was to run through his tapes of callisthenics events from previous Olympic

Games, playing and reversing the acrobatic floor exercises until his eyes became blurred. Then he would start to worry that his eyesight was deteriorating and that he might need glasses, a fate that horrified him. His concern with his own appearance verged on the obsessive. The smallest wrinkle at the edges of his eyes would drive him out for a new cream or miracle cure. His clothes became outdated in an alarmingly short time. He said that he wanted to look 'interesting in a Ralph Lauren way'. But his compulsion to discard garments after he had worn them only a few times just made him look like one more Tokyoite who sought salvation through shopping, and was therefore drowning in the same glittering sea as the rest. I started to notice that blank look of his in everyone's eyes after I got married: the mannequin-stare of all those struggling with Big-Name bags, clutching cell-phones and DVD players, slumped in subway seats, perversely hungering for a future that was not pre-designed.

I don't know where my husband would have found the money for his clothing habit if his mother had not still been supplementing his income. And now, since we had moved into the rooms on the top floor of the building housing the incense shop, he was even more centrally placed for studying the passing crowd, checking out store windows, shopping to the point of exhaustion. He was hardly alone in his slavish devotion to the Tokyo fashion scene.

No matter what recession Japan may be facing or recovering from, Tokyoites are never without the stylish carrier bags that indicate to the room, platform or street at large that they are moneyed high-achievers with impeccable taste. The paper and plastic bags my husband began to stockpile in our wardrobe were so important an accessory to his life that they were often kept far longer than the goods they originally contained. Each morning of the business week he would choose one to match his clothing and use it to ferry his *bento* box and newspaper to and from work. Granted Tokyo and suburban land prices, he had not at that stage ever contemplated buying his own home and so, as with his contemporaries, label-worship filled the need to demonstrate tangible success. It is even easier to fall into this pattern if you are one of those workers living in subsidised dormitory accommodation for which you pay relatively little rent. The employer benefits from the solidarity built up by workers never truly being outside each other's company, and the employee has a more disposable income which is poured into the quick-fix of fashion and designer goods. It's so simple a child might have devised it – as a game for other children to play. In his own bachelor days my husband might have fitted quite neatly the description of a typical 'parasite single', so-called for their tendency to remain unmarried and living at home, paying little or nothing toward rent or food. Tokyo Spends! Tokyo Lives! And at the end of it all you still have the bag to prove it.

I asked Mrs Matsu one day how she saw it from the perspective of another generation, the capacity to buy your life pre-arranged from the shelves of a department store, and then to repeat the whole process in a year's time, just for the sake of it. 'Yes,' she said with a small laugh, 'it always reminds me of the Yamonote line – round and round in the same circular pattern – except that there never seems a point where you can get off the train and continue on to your real destination. I feel I've seen so many changes in our history that I can't imagine what else could possibly happen to us. It's a small thing in itself, but when I see women these days buying expensive hand-embroidered cushions – white thread on indigo fabric – in the more prestigious gift stores, I often wonder if they know how it started. Once poor people couldn't even afford cotton clothing so they had to make do with hemp. The white cotton thread itself was a relatively precious commodity. When things were going well and they had enough thread (and some time) they would use it to make patterns on the hemp cloth, as a means of disguising what it was, of turning it into something more pleasing to the eye and closer to the cotton fabric that would have been a luxury for them. In my lifetime I've spoken to people who, in earlier times would have been overjoyed just to have had enough rice to eat each day. Now children direct that same level of longing towards the latest computer games. It's the rate of change that's sometimes the most difficult, the speeding up that moves through your world like a physical presence.'

It's true that the having of rice is no longer a problem

– not, apparently, for generations to come if one takes a look at the groaning shelves of rice in our supermarkets, a geography lesson in themselves, with every packet showing a map and a region coloured to indicate where the grain is grown, including a description of why the rice from here is the best, the most healthful of all. Like Mrs Matsu, when my mother spoke about recent history, it was not decisive military issues she considered, but the lives of ordinary people, their extraordinary powers of endurance, seemingly greater the further back one looked: the men who had to mortgage their land when the crops failed and then had to give away their grain as payment in a following bad year, instead of feeding their own families; the women who gave birth while planting rice or gathering wood, and who got up as soon as it was over and kept on with the work that had been interrupted, because they couldn't afford to do otherwise. 'It was not so long ago, in this very rich country,' she used to say, 'that people did the most extraordinary amounts of physically crippling work just to be able to have a roof over their heads, to buy rice, a cooking pot, matches. Can you imagine a life so simple that a handful of rice, or a cupful of fresh water is at times the most precious and beautiful thing you could hope for? And consider too, how many ways there would be to respond to that reality. One man might kill because of it, another write a poem. The mystery of individual human existence, the secret core, lies in the response. You need to know that at the beginning.'

I hear the cups rattling on the tray as they are taken to the kitchen in the evening, before the medication trolley does its final round. I see them in my mind's eye – their whiteness. In everyday life I never drink from a cup, only a glass. At home I drink tea from a glass in a metal holder. When I am out I buy bottled water or coffee in disposable containers. I never drink from a cup.

For our wedding my mother-in-law presented us with a pair of *meoto-jawan*, 'his-and-hers' tea-cups, prized family antiques, not intended for use but to be kept as a reminder of the husband and wife union – the pattern the same, but the wife's cup smaller. My mother-in-law was a traditionalist from the outset, a woman who would have liked to absorb a daughter-in-law into her family and then, as was once the custom, systematically mould her into a suitable partner for her son. But she was thwarted in this on a number of counts. Firstly it was her son who had entered another family by taking his wife's family name and all that that implied. Secondly, society itself was by then capable of tolerating, if not overtly embracing, a greater number of variations on 'old ways' than ever before, and I myself was not about to be redefined by anyone else's concept of who I should become. My mother-in-law and I would exchange the usual polite courtesies when we met, two minds in overdrive as the battle-lines were drawn afresh, the initial attack a seemingly discreet enquiry on her part that always ended up obliquely questioning my cooking, my housekeeping, my general suitability for the job in hand. It was obvious to her many acquaintances that she had been involved in diligently spending her late husband's resources for years, in spite of her financial adviser's warning of the effects of the recession on investments. She saw herself as a significant member of a social elite, and to admit defeat at that competitive level would no doubt have felt too much like death. My uncle, socially withdrawn and intent on the amassing and guarding of his personal fortune, was her exact opposite – the provider of necessary opportunities and future riches for her son, and a source of thin-lipped resentment, precisely because of this. I grew used to listening to her voice, initially very soft and sweet, lulling people into a state of relaxation whereby the true nature of her probing words was not analysed too much, not until after questions had been answered and information given that shifted the temporary balance of power inevitably in her direction. Typically these exchanges would take place at gatherings in the upmarket tea-rooms to be found in clothing-dominated department stores. She soon despaired of trying to draw me into her clique and I became 'the-woman-my-son-married' followed by a sad little smile.

In spite of her traditionalist tendencies, two features of western culture fascinated her almost against her will: fashion and food. She went to every fashion show to which she could obtain an invitation and spent a vast number of yen on imported fashion magazines, trying to find the 'look' that was right for her. She had a dressmaker who had been struggling with her demands for years, who would be instructed to embroider a bag or apply beading to a jacket 'just as it is in the picture', and who somehow could not help being true to her roots, thus producing a result very similar to the French or Italian or American original, but which was unmistakably Japanese in spirit. 'You see the problems I have,' my mother-in-law would sigh to me, throwing aside a wrap covered in hand-painted flowers that owed more than a little to *sumi-e* painting. 'Of course, I do have the luxury of experimenting with these things – but that has to be earned with time.' Her wardrobe bulged with discarded fashion dreams that had got to the fleeting-image stage without ever quite being realised. She and her friends would sit over their tea-cups and discuss such disappointments endlessly, exchanging worries and gossip and advice like playing cards, while they moved exquisitely constructed pastries around and around their plates with dainty forks.

Cooking – or rather, food – was my mother-in-law's other passion. Western pastries and desserts thrilled her above all else; not the taste of them so much, as the sophistication implied by their appearance. She would spend hours preparing meringue nests with spun-sugar lids presented on a bed of chocolate leaves with angelica stems, or glazed apple tarts with minute handmade apples of coloured marzipan dotted around their edges. The fact that the meringue tasted like newly-set plaster and the apple was so sickly-sweet it outdid toffee caused her no concern at all. 'This is the sort of thing you see in the window of Fauchon,' she would confide. 'I'm going to tell you the secret of how I do this, one day, when you've reached the right stage.' Curiously, despite the enormous amount of time spent choosing and ordering food, she seemed to eat very little. She would merely tweak at tiny portions with her chopsticks for what seemed like half the meal before reluctantly raising the smallest amount of food possible to her lips with an exaggerated show of delicacy. She was already reed-thin but perhaps there was a secret fear of becoming physically more sub-stantial, or did she think it a hallmark of femininity to appear to live on next to nothing, as women – particularly young wives – historically did, often being the last of all to receive nourishment, after everyone else in the family had been served?

My husband preferred to eat out with his friends as he had always done so I often had long evenings to myself. His arrival home would usually be signalled by certain predictable noises: the shuffling of footsteps as he tried to maintain his balance, a clink of metal or the soft thud of a wallet striking the ground while his keys were searched for, located and just as quickly dropped, a muttered curse or two, and finally the mouse-like scratching at the door as his key aimed wildly at the lock. Once inside he would gobble down a container of cup noodles with much slurping and grunting and sighing and fall almost immediately into a drunken sleep. And so for a second time in my life I found myself the custodian of silence, afraid of any noise that might disturb him and unleash an inevitable tirade of abuse.

It was just a question of time before he began spending whole nights away from home. I heard from a mutual acquaintance that he had been frequenting a popular Shinjuku club and that there was a girl, a very young girl whose wealthy parents were happy to indulge her every whim, and who liked to party – a lot. As far as I was concerned, our divorce was only a matter of formalities.

My husband was shocked into momentary silence when I suggested that we had made a mistake in marrying. His eyes began to move rapidly back and forth while his brow furrowed, first a little then a lot, as he realised the implications for his life as a whole. Perhaps he had visualised me as evolving into some sort of older-sister type who would scold him occasionally about his failings and indiscretions, but who would always be there in the end to pick up the pieces. What I had suggested to him implied a dramatic curtailing of his new-found freedom; for a start it meant a return to weekends of having to sit through interminable fashion shows aimed at women of his mother's generation, instead of being able to use the excuse that he had other responsibilities to attend to. He began to bluster, to excuse his recent behaviour as just letting off steam, and then he grew angry. 'You haven't mentioned any of this to your uncle, I suppose? *I'm* the son he always wanted for his business. Do you think he's going to give that up lightly because your American ideas of romance haven't been realised? Japanese women are realistic about life. They don't expect the impossible. You're a Japanese wife now. You're supposed to think about what's right for *me*, what *my* needs are . . .' And so he continued, waiting for me to back down, swinging from abuse to wheedling persuasion and back again with hardly a pause for breath. I became so exhausted by the onslaught that late into the night I lost concentration for a moment and felt myself drawing back from him, the room, even my own presence at the table. For an instant I was above, looking down, thinking how absurdly small and unnecessary it all was, and that the only possible response was silence. Eventually I fell asleep at the kitchen table, my head on my arms, the words still beating into my brain, certain only of the fact that I had not even made a choice: the end of our relationship had been there all along, in-built as a part of the whole, from the start.

My uncle was even more enraged when he heard what I had proposed. I met him alone in a park, which I considered safer than an enclosed space since I could at least walk away if the discussion got out of control.

He watched me come towards him down the path, using his eyes like daggers, trying to threaten my resolve before we had even exchanged a word. As I began to greet him he flung his cigarette down on to the gravel and ground it viciously into shards. 'This is a confirmation of everything I have been expecting. You have failed me in every way. A girl-child' – his lip curled – 'who left my home at an age when most children are looking for ways to bring credit upon their families. And now – divorce. Don't you realise how shameful divorce is? The sort of self-indulgence . . .'

Suddenly he stopped and took a step backwards, his hand reaching out for the back of a nearby seat. His breath came in short, noisy rasps that seemed to make his neck expand and contract with the effort. I moved quickly towards him but he waved me aside irritably as though he could not bear the thought of another human being recognising his vulnerability. Within minutes he had recovered enough to summon back all his former arrogance. 'I see no point in continuing this conversation. I do not wish to see or hear from you again until you can face the true nature of your responsibilities. I will send you, in writing, a statement of how things stand between us if you are unable to comply. Go – now.' After some hesitation I walked slowly away, wondering what I'd thought I could have achieved by a face-to-face meeting. I turned back once before reaching the gate, just to reassure myself he didn't need my help, and saw him still by the seat, staring down at the ground as though the haphazard patterns in the gravel had bitterly failed his expectations.

It was probably fortunate that my husband and my uncle fell out over the best way to deal with my 'difficult' nature and my decision to press ahead, as quickly as possible, for divorce. My mother-in-law initially had mixed feelings about what was going on, but the idea of welcoming home her (doubtless neglected) son for an indefinite period won the day in the end. And if there was a young and wealthy Japanese girlfriend in the background, well, he could hardly be blamed ... And so in the end our parting came to seem like an inevitability, not only to me, but to everyone concerned.

In the thirteenth century a woman wishing to leave her husband had to flee the family home and enter a *kakekomi-dera*, a refuge temple where she would lead the rigorous spartan life of a nun and be safe from threats and persecution. She was not free to remarry or have contact with her children until three years had passed, or until her husband consented to divorce. It took until 1873, six centuries later, for a law to be passed allowing Japanese women to instigate divorce proceedings themselves.

❋

Whenever I met Mrs Matsu, instead of directly enquiring how I was, she had the habit of asking,

'And how is your brushwork today?' and the implication of her question was also that painting was a normal part of the human experience, a way of being, of growing. I believe she could tell everything she needed to know about someone from a single stroke of a brush on paper: the degree of happiness or sadness, a love of life, a desire to end life . . . In spite of the fact that it was normal, in the long tradition of Chinese and Japanese painting, to recreate the great works from the past, forgeries did exist in their own right. She could tell instantly, by a fragment of brushwork, if she was looking at an imitation of the real thing. 'See, here, it's too considered,' or 'It's been put down carelessly,' or 'It tails off too quickly,' and her infallible eye would work back along the line, knowing that the heart was not in it.

When I told her of my impending divorce she seemed not at all surprised. She took me into her small garden and we inspected the cuttings and shoots and small plants that had come her way. 'Look,' she said, pointing to one thriving specimen that had recently been given to her by a neighbour, 'last week this was half-dead. Now, it will be flowering soon, I think.'

And so I am again a 'free' woman, which is to say, relatively free, given the constraints of the society where I have spent so much of my life. Relatively free too, in Tokyo, the multi-faced city where one more woman who has rationalised her life is neither here nor there. It might be a different matter in a country town or a small community where everyone knows you and your family. There are many places still where you can find discrimination against those who ease themselves free of one of the practically inevitable blobs of social glue. It is seen as potentially disrupting stability. What if everyone did it? Or re-thought their earlier decisions at all kinds of other levels? But they don't. The ties-that-bind, and then the glue, and then a cling-film wrap at a store of your choice, and you're well on your way to going round and round, as it was intended you should do. And yet suddenly I have stopped. Long enough to think. Or at least long enough to begin listening to what other lives are being lived out there. One part of me says my life is here, has always really been and will remain here, and another part of me asks, Why? Why not travel now as I always secretly wanted to do? The sense of facing a journey, of facing in all directions at once. Needing the courage to go, to stay.

This was the point at which my evenings began to be shaped by the meetings in the room above the incense shop. The hours when I again came to be called Sei Shōnagon, for my capacity to recall the past. The difference this time was the way in which the present seemed to intrude on the stories of history, as though a gently-plucked instrument of the ancient court was being drowned out by a collective cry of unstoppable pain.

I remember being half-awake sometimes when an intense blue would begin to saturate the strip of glass visible between the curtains. It became, in my semi-dream, a colour I wanted to know. If I had only been able to reach out and draw it to me, let it flow around my pillows and sink into the white sheets and finally fill my mind with blue light, then I knew I would at last sleep deeply, and wake later, renewed, with no memories of the shadows that lurk in dreams.

He first came to me as if through a garden. That is what we spoke of, in the beginning. The mystery of its workings, the way you carry something of it with you when you are a traveller, until you can set the ideas and the longing for its space down again somewhere, and step into it, and be, utterly still.

Gardens are not why he came here but they have captured him nevertheless. I asked him if he didn't think he was in the wrong city. Kyoto is the home of the Japanese garden, after all. Yes, yes, he agrees. But surely the greater impact is here, in Tokyo? The moment when it stops. It's that moment when the high-pitched impassive scream of the city just . . . stops. That's what fascinates him. A sudden path of irregular stones, trees, a single slab forming a bridge, sunlight on water, a flash of red-gold beneath, a rising up of rocks, a waterfall. The shock hitting you between the shoulder blades. The way the body unclenches. He still can't get over it. These gardens blossoming like exquisite flowers in a steel trap. He would like to photograph each stone laid to receive a foot because he can see, in the choosing and placement, a mind that saw the whole in the particular. A philosophy expressed by a pathway, in the picking up and the putting down of stone.

His name is Alain. A photographer come to Japan from France, to write about the otherness of this country in images. Wanting information from me about other ages, our history, our thinking, who we are. We quickly fall into a pattern of communicating in English and French and long pauses. There are some insurmountable difficulties of translation, Japanese words for which there is no direct equivalent. His hand gestures, glimpsed from behind my screen, instinctively provoke a similar response in me when the words won't fit or are simply absent. Thus we sit, with the screen between us, our hands opening, rising, gesturing, falling, as though to pluck words from the fragrant air itself.

I tell him we do not have enough hours, enough days, to cover everything he has asked about. Could he not get what he needs from books, reference materials? There is so much available today, in so many languages, and the major bookstores of Tokyo are vast ...

'But that would be like preparing to make a portrait

of someone without a personal meeting. It's not only what you know. It's also what you choose to tell me, what strikes you as important on a given day. I've spent a lot of my life looking in – into a lens, dipping into other worlds, running in small circles sometimes, just to meet deadlines. Since I've arrived here I've been overcome by a desire to take whatever time is needed – as long as it takes – to do this work. And I want the luxury of looking out, through the eyes of someone who belongs here.'

'How ironic that you should have chosen me.'

'I'm sorry, you spoke so quietly that I . . .'

'It is of no consequence. I think I understand what you are looking for. I would only wish to add that, in my opinion, you might still be underestimating the time you will need to do this in the way you have described. You told me earlier that you felt your understanding of what you saw had to be informed by a knowledge of the history behind it. It would take a lifetime to fill in the background – the true historical context – you require. And besides, I am an amateur, intrigued far more by colours and textures and moods than by exact dates or the debatable accuracy of certain early texts. Are you sure you wouldn't rather begin by talking to an historian?'

'No. I believe what I want to know will be immeasurably enhanced by the perspective you bring to it, and by the fact that you have been absorbing all of these things since you were a small child – for your whole lifetime to date.'

'Do you take many portraits?'

'Yes.'

'How long does it normally take to make a good photographic portrait?'

'A lifetime.'

The meetings between us continue, become more frequent, in spite of my misgivings. I rationalise that, after all, he will not be here forever. I simply have to wait it out. Wait for a slight unexpected fever to pass. I don't like admitting so much to myself.

As long as I remain behind the screen.

He questions everything: 'May I ask you something else?'

'Of course.'

'When do you stop listening to others and take time out for yourself?'

'I have a very full life. Please don't worry about me.'

'Mmm . . . You will have to forgive this unpardonable breach of etiquette but, for example, do you ever, perhaps sing or dance purely for the pleasure of it – do anything unplanned, just for the sake of enjoying a sense of Being?'

'I am not unhappy. I wonder where you got that idea.'

'I didn't mention unhappiness. I just feel that I'm looking at an incredibly organised life – your life – where every minute seems to be planned, and I'm . . . wondering a little. Well, wondering more than I usually would. Surprising myself for once. I am aware from my own experience that involvement in the lives of others can become a means of self-avoidance, the ultimate escape.'

'I'm not trying to escape from anything, I assure you. I simply know who I am.'

'The way you say it – it sounds somehow static, finished.'

'Perhaps the cultural norms are simply too different. It seems to me there are huge differences between our lives in every respect.'

'I realise I'm being unspeakably impolite. Not to mention doing exactly what I'm accusing you of doing – except of course I'm not escaping into your problems, merely making a gentle enquiry or two ... So, you are not escaping from anything? Extraordinary. In the west we are always running away from something. It's the degree of it that matters. An excessive level of escape is cause for concern, although if it makes enough serious money we learn to live with it and call it a career. Dare I hope for a smile?'

'I refuse to encourage you.'

'All right, just grant me this: I'd like a clue as to your likes and dislikes away from this room. I don't know what is really celebrated here, although in a city known for its temples and shrines you also do Christmas more thoroughly than Paris. What did you hope for, say, for last Christmas, or its equivalent here?'

A pause.

'The skill to make a painting that was true enough to enter. And you?'

'For Christmas? After what I've seen of the world?
... Peace, and love.'

The language of gifts. Christmas is only one of our
many gift-giving times. Is it a love of ceremony, or an
apology for the inability to express emotion and
gratitude with easy grace? A learned dependence on
formal gestures is the downside of our increasingly
polite society.

The light patterns shift across my eyelids, day sliding
into night and back again into another dawn.

I recall meeting Yuko, an old university friend, for a
quick lunch. She smiles with exactly the same wry
twist of her lips as always; her 'ironic face' we used to
say, teasing her because she seemed the most analytical
and detached of us all. She has married since we last
met – a well-established businessman and long-time
friend of her parents. After our snack at a noodle bar
we set off on a mission: Yuko has to return home with
an anniversary gift for her in-laws and something
appropriate for her husband to present to a visiting
colleague from overseas. 'I don't know,' she says
quietly as we examine a presentation basket containing one perfect melon surrounded by glowing ruby
grapes, 'I think I'm losing the ability to make choices.
I used to be quite good at this sort of thing, but these
days ...'

She still runs her own design business despite gentle but ongoing pressure from her husband's family to concentrate on home and social commitments. 'Sometimes I think it's like gas escaping from a pipe,' she says. 'A little more of it enters the atmosphere each day and you wonder how long it will be before you go under.' So far she has also managed to maintain her tiny sculpture studio with sheets draping the work-in-progress, but the dust is gathering.

We locate a store dealing in antiques and specialised crafts from all walks of life. What an industrious and skilled people we have been, century after century — cutting and carving and shaping and forging and plaiting and weaving and embroidering.

A tiny carved cicada on a piece of bamboo, a jade butterfly, an indigo jacket, a fan with painted dragon-flies in a summer sky. Will it all come to an end one day when these things are bought and squirrelled away? At the back of the store there is an exhibition space with a man bent low over his table, working on one of several wood-blocks that together will make a multi-coloured print. His face is expressionless but the eyes, flashing towards a gathering audience, harden briefly before moving back to the work. Yes, they say in a glance, I'm skilled. No, the pay is not good and I still have to eat in this city and find the rent. No, my son won't be following me. He's going into IT.

Alain continues to visit the room above the incense shop to ask his questions.

I tell him about the court, the ceremonies, the pavilions, the gardens.

'A stream or river should move through its created landscape as does a dragon. The house should be built in the curve of the river where the stomach of the dragon lies . . .

'In the tension between water and earth, water can erode, but earth can define direction. If earth chooses, it can stop the flow of water; if water chooses, it can flood the earth . . .'

'I seem to be separated from you many times over. Is this necessary?'

'Yes. The screen is a part of this. Perversely, I believe you can hear my voice more clearly that way.'

'And what is the scent in this room?'

'*Kyara*, one of the most precious of the *jinkoh* fragrances. Close your eyes and listen to it.'

'Why "listen"?'

'This is how we speak of it. By now, no one can be certain of its origins. The term began to be used by us sometime in the fifteenth century – borrowed from the Chinese *Wenxiang* – but the idea goes right back to early Buddhist scriptures where the words for fragrance and incense are the same. In a discussion between a Bodhisattva and an Indian Buddhist layman it is revealed that the essence of all things in the world of Buddha can be conveyed by fragrance or incense, including Buddha's words. And so the inhaling of incense was also a way of listening to Buddha.'

'Sometimes one must stop before one can "listen" in any form, and I seem to have been part of a world of continuous activity for a very long time.'

'Yes, but then too, there are many ways of listening.'

'As many as the ways of seeing? The Heian diaries . . . The writers seem so selective about their subject matter. What about life outside the court? Did they know or care anything about it?'

'That's a question people have been debating for a very long time. I think I would say this: I believe that just as language can be used as a means of exclusion equally as well as a means of communication, so some notebooks were written not necessarily to reveal an entire range of thoughts, impressions and feelings, but to selectively conceal them.

'It could, for example, be construed that if you wrote extensively about the endless round of games, ceremonies and minor excursions – a life obsessed with hairstyles and fabrics and gift-giving – then you were no threat to a social order that considered itself a virtual religion. If you appeared to subscribe fervently enough to a set number of given attitudes, then your overall compliance to the status quo could be assumed. Thus your individuality, whatever form it actually took, would not be read as subversive. In some ways of course it could be, but within expected limits this was tolerated. It was expected, for example, that the ladies of the court could entertain visitors when they chose, and that they would have lovers. (Servants had to know about them in order not to lock the gates at night, in order not to intrude.) Discretion and social propriety were nominally maintained as long as the man left by dawn, not forgetting, incidentally, to write and send a poem in which he deeply regretted the parting, as soon as he reached his own home. To neglect to do this was either an unpardonable breach of etiquette or could be read as an extreme lack of interest. So, as long as the agreed formulas were adhered to, people of a certain rank had some choices and freedoms that would be unimaginable at other times. I'm thinking particularly of a story I heard, of a certain upper-class situation, centuries after the Heian period had finished, where a boy and a girl – teenage children – could be forced to commit ritual suicide because they had been discovered talking quietly together, alone in a room. The outrageousness of the crime consisted in going against the norms of their time.'

'And outside the court? There seems to be so much one can only guess at.'

'Outside the protective walls of the Heian court were terrible things. Secretly we knew that. We were faced with only two ways of looking at it: either those "others" were of a different order altogether – almost another species – or they were, as Buddhists, acquiring credit for their next incarnation (or possibly expiating sins from a previous one). Each world was in its way a sealed unit. Within the walls there was personal power of a significant but limited nature, the power of indulged dolls inside their paper and bamboo dolls' houses, the whole again inside the stone walls of a castle that lay in the midst of what could be a savage and terrible landscape. A place where men, women and children regularly died of overwork and malnutrition. Infanticide was as common then as it was in China or India. Families wanted sons. Girl children born during a "Year of the Horse" were popularly believed to be capable of consuming their husbands, and so were even more vulnerable than usual to being smothered at birth. The method remained a standard means of birth control through centuries. At the end of the nineteenth century there was the case of a girl who was asphyxiated soon after she was born and then left by the hearth until morning. Miraculously she revived, and the family was so aghast at what they saw as supernatural intervention that they let her live and later, when she was old enough to understand, told her all about it.

'In our beautifully-landscaped Heian world the bones of all the sisters we denied waited just beyond the farthest grove of plum trees, their ghosts rising in the night to travel along water courses, to pass through shutters as a cold wind. It was only at dawn we could deny the shadow-play they made from dreamed whispers; then we would wake quickly and call for the reddest cloaks to drive out the chill, the brightest

125

lamps to fill our rooms with certainty. We reached for colour as for a drug. Although we praised snow in our poetry, it had about it a silence in which one could start to question everything, and, in its utter absence of colour, a reminder of the whiteness of death.'

When he photographs trees he aims his lens high up into the branches. He is only interested in the way the black skeleton breaks up the space. Some photographers 'construct' their images, but he prefers to pare everything back to the most basic poetry there is. Later he was to show me a western view of Tokyo – a Braque palette, Miró shapes, Picasso scaffolding, Rothko paper – and then turn his camera to the trees and give me ink-washed skies, a drift of *sumi-e* blossom like a flight of birds and 'petals on a wet, black bough'.

If you have never been to Tokyo in spring it is hard to visualise what happens to interrupt the normally grey-clad city on its seemingly endless commute to and from work. *Hanami* is what happens – blossom viewing. And miraculously something also seems to open inside people, inside even the sternest and most work-oriented of businessmen. *Hanami* is like a whisper that overnight becomes a song. Women begin by wearing the palest pinks and yellows and greens. The cherry blossom symbolises the brief, beautiful flowering of a life and for us has always seemed to encapsulate a very particular Japanese sense of sadness. But for the few days that the cherry blooms, the indifference and cynicism of a vast city are softened. Strangers smile at each other as they encounter a playground that children might have invented – a slow explosion of shell-pink light, a dream-world, absurdly unsophisticated, with weighted boughs nodding before cool-eyed office blocks. And yet, more than the trees, it is the air itself that seems transformed; sunlight filtered through a screen of petals changes everything, turns businessmen from aggressive major players into fellow-members of an audience – husbands and fathers and friends, out on a late-afternoon picnic. And for that short time everyone is briefly born again, more luminous than would have seemed possible a week before, released from greyness. Above all it is the season of the feminine, of the earth mother and her daughter, and as each Japanese Persephone rises up from her commute through subway hell, she knows that this is all to do with her; she lifts her head, opens her hands, and spring blossoms where she walks.

I cannot resist buying paper in spring, particularly the creamy white cards and writing sheets with their delicate smattering of blossoms or petals. We are a seasonal people. Come the end of spring these papers disappear completely and fans and new cotton fabrics fill the shop windows along with images of full moons and cicadas and golden fish. In some Tokyo stores you will find entire floors devoted to paper – handmade, calligraphy, coloured, embossed, lacy, translucent, printed or painted – granted the space and reverence other cultures give to luxury jewellery. It seems no matter what we do we will continue to be viewed as a nation of paper by the rest of the world, tied to it as the Swiss are bound to the watch. And so we continue to fold it, twist it and plait it into ropes, wrap it around our endless compulsory gifts to each other, make doors and windows from it and use the sunlight filtered through it to reveal the true qualities of woodblock prints, which is of course, how they were always intended to be seen.

And now there is Alain. A Frenchman who feels less so every time he returns to what once was home. Who wonders why he thrives so much more outside his own territory, apparently the further away the better.

He tells me about his first serious opportunity – Beijing, a year after Tiananmen Square. The people still reticent, some afraid even to be seen giving him directions; others recklessly glad to meet someone from 'outside', letting him photograph their children, asking him to pose with their relatives. (For years he wondered if there would be any repercussions when their films were developed.) His best subject was a child, smiling shyly at him at first, over its mother's shoulder, as he followed them all the way down

Wanfujing Street, he dodging between shoppers, trying to get the face into focus, the infant's grin rapidly widening as the game of hide and seek grew more complex, the rakish red woollen beret bobbing above the huge eyes, above the red of the mother's cardigan – red, the colour of luck and happiness. Around him people turned and smiled, no language problem, no cultural differences: he is photographing our children; this is natural, they are the most beautiful children in the world . . .

It was not so easy perhaps for a few onlookers to understand why he was photographing a couple of tin mugs on a peeling wooden bench. But that was China too, and they were also beautiful, the muted colours and the shapes. Everything he saw struck his eye as right – the carved door panels, pale jade jewellery framed by the softened red of old woodwork, even the piles of vegetables. It all belonged in a way that gave him a momentary sense of almost physical pain. In a narrow lane leading to the Summer Palace he found a courtyard containing an ancient bike and, balanced on a ledge, two scarlet slippers, a Chinese version of *The Red Shoes*, looking as though they could fly out the gate at any minute and pick their way down the dusty road like the delicate echo of some fading song. In the public gardens of what had once been private palaces, old men took their caged birds for an early evening stroll, while others calmly did *t'ai chi* exercises, or simply sat and meditated. He was grateful for the fact that when his shutter clicked it did so quietly, more often than not lost among the pinging bicycle bells and the unselfconscious chatter of children and birds. He walked everywhere, had whole conversations with people and later realised the absence of a common language hadn't mattered at all. He was young and intrusive and only knew how much so when an elderly man he had been aiming at with a long-range lens, suddenly raised his head from his book, gazed at the camera and at him for a long while, and then looked away.

Before he began to travel he promised himself he would not become a collector of things. There would just be him and his essential photographic equipment. But this first time there was a small jade sea-goddess rising from the waves – a green like water stilled for a moment, a figure that had been waiting inside the stone when it had been part of a landscape. Like his cameras it came to represent home to him, but unlike them it did not travel with him but stayed wherever his nominal base was, the gentle reminder that another job had just been completed, that he could rest now, have a few long, slow breakfasts, read a book or two, to rest his eyes.

And so we also discovered a shared fascination with the enigma of jade: its coolness in the hand, which has the effect of calming the whole being, its range of colours and hues, its centuries-old capacity to inspire both exceptional creativity and great cruelty; the element of luck in selecting the boulder at source – trying to predict the seam of precious colour before the split is made, before a fortune is won or lost; the element of fate in how you may otherwise come to know the stone – wearing an exquisite pendant around your neck, or dying, as you search for the raw material in a Burmese mining camp.

I smell apples. Someone in the hospital has been given a basket of apples. I can taste their sharp sweetness in the scent that hangs in the air just beyond my nose, my mouth, my closed eyes. I long for an apple. I swallow the scent instead, and feel half-tears pricking against my eyelids. As a child new to Japan I had inwardly fretted at my own sense of powerlessness. Now, I would give anything just to be able to raise a piece of fruit to my lips.

Alain once told me about the apple orchard behind his family home and how they would store the harvest upstairs in the *grenier*, a room that held the aroma of fruit all the year round. 'When I was a boy, the creak on the seventh step combined with the scent of apples gave me the greatest pleasure you could imagine, a sense of release from any thing in the day that had been trivial and constraining.'

When he'd moved to Paris he'd thought he would be able to go home at weekends and have the best of both worlds, but it didn't work out that way. The only quiet moments he could snatch from the week were walks by the Seine in the pearl-grey of early morning. Inevitably this led to thoughts of other rivers, other cities he had read about but never seen. Then one day, without thinking about it too much, he went to China on a photography assignment and finally stood atop the river of stone called the Great Wall and felt like a time traveller. No going back. When Alain returned from China he was surprised how long it took to readjust to western cities. So much appeared superfluous after what he had just witnessed. The force of his discomfort felt like a wake-up call. He had never actually rebelled against a conservative middle-class lifestyle, just drifted. It wasn't until his return from China that he realised how far.

Some believe that if people are denied possessions or talismans of any kind, they can lose a sense of personal identity. The question: deciding how much baggage is necessary for your own particular journey. A need to recognise at what point you cease to be strengthened by ownership and instead become imprisoned by it.

Following Beijing Alain went to Istanbul – after centuries of intrigue, rebellion and bloodshed, still a great centre of trade. Labyrinthine markets, tiny shops, markets containing a thousand shops and inside each shop, a market. In the mornings he grew used to passing labourers waking up on the building sites where they slept and ate and eked out precarious lives while they tried to save money to send home to Anatolia. It was said that there was serious money to be made in the building trade. It was also said that the proportion of sand used in the cement was too high and that one day there'd be a tragedy.

His zigzag between France and the rest of world, between tragedies-just-been, and those in waiting. Perhaps the photographer sees himself as a moving target in the end, trying to avoid some invisible larger lens that's always waiting, fixed on him.

The tasks behind the day-to-day running of the incense shop had quickly become second nature to me and I would often move seamlessly between chores in the back office and storage rooms, hardly noticing that minutes had passed into hours. While I enjoyed my usual behind-the-scenes role, my preferred moment of the day came after closing time when I could wander around the store at leisure, adjusting the displays and sampling the assorted scents for my own pleasure. Whether it was a long-standing favourite in the form of an incense stick or a pinch of some new mixture held within the folded petals of a paper flower, I would inhale and register each fragrance in turn, feeling as though I were stealing through a garden of rare and secret delights.

The last window display I remember creating for the shop involved a low black platform on which stood a shallow bowl of bluish-green porcelain. A hidden fan sent fine ripples across the liquid in the bowl, setting in motion two creamy-white flowers that almost seemed to hover above the surface of the water. Around the bowl they drifted, towards each other and then apart, slow dancers in a private ballet that continued until the sky darkened and they grew still, luminous and slightly unearthly in the moonlight.

I left America when I was seven years old. Just enough time to get used to the idea that there were many ways of looking at life. Of living. But perhaps I had grown more Japanese than I had realised, thinking all the while that I was simply wearing a mask of social compliance in order to survive.

No maps for when I met him. The shock of suddenly looking deeply into another person forcing me at the same time to look deeply into myself. The desire not to do so. And then the chaos of so many things coming towards me in a rush.

In the end it's always the eyes that give you away. I waited behind my screen for him to grow tired of the novelty of our meetings and to move on, secure in my anonymity, toasting my victory in jasmine tea after each encounter – calmness, coolness, detachment. And then I would feel the pulse in my neck.

He waited for me.

There were no plans for this to happen in my life when it did, but like the beautiful economy of haiku, it did not allow itself to be analysed or logically appraised; it was simply there, a truth like white light.

This is how he loved me:

A hand passing down the arm of a kimono, as wind might sing to water.

In the history of our gardens there is the recurring image of an island. The meeting of mountain and sea. The ancient Chinese believed that the five Isles of the Blessed were to be found somewhere far off the east coast of China. These islands were said to be the dwelling place of the Immortals, who flew around their mountain peaks on the backs of cranes. A world of peace beyond anything known.

This is how he loved me:

Lying down on me as gently as snow falls to other snow.

The search for the Elixir of Immortality runs like a thread through Chinese history, representing so many things to so many people, even an end to wanting itself. The Taoists, as a last resort, turned to Alchemy to assist them, but were disappointed like the rest. The search became the stuff of dreams and then of myth. By the first century Emperor Wu of Han had ceased to have faith in expeditions and embarked on a more subtle plan. He decided to draw the Gods to him instead, by designing a paradise worthy of them, created from the elements of his own world.

This is how he loved me:

A blackness of eyes in the half-light – so shocked

with wanting, so intent that he does nothing else, does not even breathe. And then the moment of breathing me in, that has no end.

How much later it was that we went to the island in the Inland Sea, I can't quite remember. The weather was beautiful (of course it was – everything, beautiful). I felt so alive I was embarrassed to walk down the street because I thought people would read my face and be affronted because I could not hide my feelings sufficiently. This was when we took time off – serious time off – and went to an island far away from Tokyo, in western Japan. There was a train to Okayama, I recall, with a mountain approaching fast as we looked from the window, the colours changing purple to blue to blue-green, and then a rising mist as sudden as dragon's breath. And afterwards the wooden boat, a quiet lapping of waves. We had rented a friend's tiny holiday house – the utter luxury of privacy – and for the first few days, unused to the silence, hardly believing our freedom, we jumped at every unfamiliar noise, as though we were guilty of trespassing. There was a single shop – apples, rice, eggs, bananas, brandy. That was it. That did very well with the fish we caught and grilled down on the beach. I can relive every moment of those evenings, the feel of cool sand, the heightened taste of everything in the sea air, my skin's

awareness of the scarf around my neck. My skin's
awareness . . .

It is dark and quiet. Probably it is the middle of the
hospital night. Somewhere, someone will be wondering
if it is too early to start writing reports on the more
stable patients, or checking a watch to confirm if it is
time to do another round. There is a door banging at
the end of the corridor. Banging its way insistently
into my brain. Forcing me to remember the last
evening, before here. Alain was overseas on another
assignment, and I was in the process of winding up my
'evenings'. There were still, however, a few people who
insisted on keeping their appointments over the next
couple of weeks, and so I had agreed.

I saw Mr F. only once.
   A clothing designer happily married for forty years
to one of his first models.
   'You can't imagine how beautiful she was. I don't
know how much I really loved her then, at the
beginning, or whether, in the way of young men, I just
wanted her unbearably and told myself it must be love
to be so powerful. And there too, timing counts for so

much, doesn't it? There is a certain time when everything comes together, and overnight your life turns into a French Revolution on its own account. (Is that how all men end up marrying?) Of course, I grew to love her seriously over the years. The trouble was, I found I wanted them both – the more interesting woman and companion as well as the unattainable exquisite young girl I had first seen modelling kimono in my own early days. I wanted her to mature and I wanted her unchanged, just as I wanted my own wealth and experience to accompany the strong confident young hero I had once imagined myself to be. My models now are still beautiful as only young Japanese girls can be: heartbreaking in their innocence, flawless skin, luminous eyes – and their hair . . . They see me as a courteous old-world-type, a father figure. They hug me, show me pictures of their holidays, their boyfriends. They trust me. The tension becomes almost unbearable sometimes.

'I have taught myself to switch off, at least when I am with my models. I couldn't bear them to think of me as anything other than the employer they trust. And I have the bitter compensation of now and again feeling their arms about my neck – the smoothness of that skin, their lips brushing my cheek. You see, I have my two-edged sword, as my reward for good behaviour. And meanwhile my wife, this other "me" who now runs a modelling agency in her own right, has become the mirror I dread as well as love. Her face reminds me too much of my own age, my own morbidity. Does she suspect that when I close my eyes and caress her shoulder I am making love to someone else entirely? How many women know the point at which this starts to happen? It's true of course, that many Japanese women are pragmatic about marriage. Perhaps for them it would not be of such great significance. But I know my wife was in love when we married and for someone like her it is a lifetime thing in every way. What would she feel if she knew what went through my mind? Although I'm hardly the worst of the bunch if you consider the kinds of films we make all the time, the "men's *manga*" that even kids read. The trouble is, it's a cumulative influence – so much available on the screen and the page but then you mustn't . . . And yet, wherever you look, they are out there, the female of the species, exquisitely presented for us like sweetmeats in a box. So enticing. So silent.

'It's the fact that I know exactly what I can and can't get away with – that's where the problems start. When I'm at work I can put everything on hold, become the complete professional, because for me at least, the consequences of doing otherwise don't bear thinking about. I know some men get away with murder, but if I should lose credibility then the industry gossip would make me a laughing stock. That's enough to dampen the most ardent enthusiasm, I can tell you. I just have to imagine that overall scenario and I can get on with the job and go no further than playing the kind uncle. Up to a point, you see, the self-control technique works for me.

'What doesn't work is being suddenly released by anonymity. Something gives way when I am just another traveller in a train carriage. Those dewy-eyed little girls everywhere, those faces saying nothing more than, "Please like me: I make my face up like a doll for you, I wear these tiny skirts so you can appreciate my legs, I giggle like a child so you will find me endearing. I long for your approval, for your validation of my worth – please, please like me." And I do. I like them so much it's become an addiction. I almost slip into a trance as I watch them on that long journey home, the motion of the train, the tantalising way their hair falls forward over their faces, the bare legs that are so close, and everywhere you look, soft curves pushing out fabric . . . And so I have become the thing I most despise. I wait for peak-time, when I know the trains will be packed. I patrol the platform methodically, watching out for the sweet face with the frequently downcast eyes, the demure one who will be too embarrassed to make a fuss, who will eventually just remove herself to another carriage or train, to avoid the dreadful attention that would follow any cry or accusation she made. I am an expert at it.

'I know I am one of many.

'Do they really think a campaign of anti-harassment posters will stop us?'

He leaves abruptly after telling me these things while I remain seated behind the screen, trying to find something else to focus on, something to centre me. And then I press a hand to my belly and remember that you are now at the centre of my being, my focus. And I tell you, to reassure both of us, that your father Alain will be back soon and I will be able to tell him even more about you.

He did not want to go on this latest assignment. But his destiny has not been that of a cautious man and it is not for me to change that in him. I even hesitated about telling him the news, my news – ours. I wasn't certain what he would say. In the end he said nothing. Just held me, and looked incredulous for a long while as though a miracle had happened, and held me again and then at arms' length and finally he gave a wonderful soft laugh and we both laughed together, as though we were caught unawares seeing sunlight for the first time.

That last evening we spent together we talked about everything at random, as though we had to say it all there and then – books and films and music and food, places we would see together and people we had known. How a chance meeting with one individual could sometimes bring a culture alive for you in a few moments. I spoke about my first meeting with Mrs Matsu, the way she had led me out of a closed world and into an unfolding one through painting. Alain told me about a shoe-shine boy who had followed him around Istanbul, badgering him for details about a life in photography. In one country a boy of nine or ten sits down to afternoon tea while a mother restrains herself from brushing hair out of his eyes; in another country he hoists his tools of trade more firmly on to his shoulder and tries to plan his next career move. In some countries the next move can only be an army.

The element of chance. In meetings, partings. Moments isolated in a giant lens. The gift of life given in the second it takes you to step back one pace on a platform, or taken, as you are dazzled by a car shooting out of the darkness.

After Mr F. had gone down the stairs I heard the door bang, loudly, quickly, as though he was running from something. As though he was trying to leave a part of himself shut in behind the door. I should have gone down to lock it. I intended to, but just for a moment I needed to sit quietly there, behind the screen, trying to put my thoughts in order. I heard a short, brusque knock far below and then the faint creak of the hinge. A heavy tread on the stair.

I came out from behind the screen to find my uncle standing in the middle of the room, his face contorted with hatred. I had not seen him since our previous disastrous meeting in the park, and had assumed, following a curt note from him after my divorce over a year ago, that the damage done was irreparable.

Suddenly I am seven years old again. I remember that I always thought of him as an agent of darkness, perhaps because I was always facing windows, turned towards the source of light, and he, by inclination, would turn in the opposite direction, his back to the sunlight, blocking it off. I remembered the way he would sometimes dress in samurai attire, the two swords hanging from his left shoulder, a symbol of honour he would never deserve in real life. Predictably he loved movies that dealt with the exploits of warrior heroes, and his own collection was vast. He was even more surly with my mother and me after watching one of these (which he always did in isolation), and would even wake my mother up with an imperious shout if the hour were late, to demand tea or a series of snacks. So many memories lay buried: images came back to me, rapidly one after another, with the shock of seeing him so unexpectedly standing there. He was the black wall, the screen on to which the past flashed in broken fragments. Perhaps I had not even admitted to myself the extent of the relief I had felt when I had received that last note from him, which stated in coldly polite phrases that the break between us was final, utterly irrevocable.

Oddly, I almost expected him to begin questioning me about the history of the sword. The old childish sense of panic rose up in me again even as I tried to suppress it. The metals – what was it about the metals that was so important? And the periods, so neatly divided up; was history ever so neat anywhere, as it was portrayed in history books?

A sudden stillness came over his face and he lifted his head as though looking down on me from a great height. At the back of my mind I remember thinking that if I was to avert some terrible disaster I would have to seize control of the situation then, at that very moment. But I was paralysed. I waited for him to speak, instead of challenging him with my eyes, instead of demanding an explanation as to why he had entered my home in that manner. His voice, when he spoke, was oddly restrained, reminding me of water gushing from a broken dam somewhere in the distance, growing steadily louder and more uncontrollable with every passing second, finally doing nothing but sweeping all to oblivion as it overwhelmed whatever lay in its path.

He knew about the baby. A series of simple coincidences had led to the knowledge being briefly noted at the local ante-natal clinic where I had recently had an appointment, mentioned, as such things are from one friend to another, passed on to him as congratulations by a distant acquaintance who knew of my marriage but not the subsequent divorce, and had assumed he would be delighted to have a new addition to the family. In another age, he told me, I would have died for my folly as I deserved. I tried to move back as he came towards me, the stream of abuse growing louder until it was an incoherent throbbing of noise that stopped all thought.

The door at the end of the ward bangs. He comes towards me. The door bangs. If only someone would shut it, perhaps the blow will not fall. I can't remember the moment of it happening, but it must have all the same. Perhaps I was searching, as I suddenly realised I must do, for something to put between us, but in all the lovely emptiness of that room, the emptiness that is so Japanese in its beauty, there was nothing, just a screen, and a fan lying on the floor. And then with horrible suddenness I see myself looking straight at the fan, lying on the same level as it, watching a red fish swim towards me. There is silence everywhere as, in a single seamless movement, the fish turns into a small river, a shiny red river, that starts to soak slowly into the tiny spaces between the tightly-packed fibres of the *tatami*. There is a sweet metallic taste in my mouth and it seems to be a long time before I connect the blood in my mouth with the little river on the floor, and then night starts to fall over the river and the *tatami* fields it is irrigating and hours later, so it seems, there is a siren in the distance, and I am surprised at the sound because it seems we must surely be in the countryside where such noises are rare and I have been lying on the ground for far too long – my body has gone to sleep, completely.

Mrs Matsu has been coming to see me.

She is by the bed again, holding my hand, willing me back to movement and speech. She has heard that some people can recover if they are not allowed to drift further into that unconscious world, if the thread to reality is maintained by words, if they are not allowed to forget their lives. She talks about everything that I have learnt, done, seen with her. And then she brings out the letter from Alain, dated more than ten days ago when I could still walk and speak and visualise a life stretching out before us. I sense there is something troubling her as she begins to read his unfolding story of an exploratory trip into eastern Turkey in search of their Kurdish contact.

I am writing this by moonlight. (Not nearly as romantic as it sounds – temperatures drop suddenly here at night and our jeep has broken down.) There is a town visible up ahead but we will wait until daybreak before approaching it so as not to alarm anyone.

We were just loading up again yesterday after an overnight stop when a truck backed over the pack containing our medical supplies, torches and the mobile phones (luckily not the cameras!). So no calls back home until we sort something out. The driver is interpreter, diplomat and scout all rolled into one, a saviour under present circumstances, if a little paranoid – he thinks we're being followed. I will write again when I can.

Mrs Matsu pauses as if her mind is momentarily elsewhere.

'Perhaps he'll be back soon,' she says. And there is silence for a while.

It is another day and then another, but despite the slow passage of time, no more news of Alain. Mrs Matsu arrives once again bringing me her bulletins of the outside world. There are things between us that we have, at one time or another, discussed exhaustively. There are things we have never discussed at all. It slips out quietly on one of her visits, as if it is just another piece of news among the rest: 'I meant to tell you also, your uncle has been very ill, has had a severe heart attack. He was not found for some time and they don't ... it is unlikely ... But the main thing is that *you* are going to get well. That is all we must focus on now.'

He has had a heart attack.

Her voice grows quieter, almost a whisper, as though she is talking to herself. 'I know about what happened when you were a child, although we have never spoken of it aloud. You were so closed-in when I first met you, I thought we would see, I would wait for you to tell me, and if you didn't, then perhaps that meant you wanted to put it completely out of your mind, and maybe that was best. But it was no accident that brought me to you as a teacher and a friend ...'

Somehow I know what she will say next, but I don't want to hear the words. I don't want to relive what happened after my mother died. If I could raise a hand or open my mouth I could stop her, but I can't do anything at all. I can't even stop my own mind from slipping towards a symbol of terror that has always reappeared whenever I have been very frightened.

I am falling backwards and the masks are coming at

me from all angles. Terrible masks that are still waiting to be finished, hanging like inhuman remains from every inch of the mask maker's wall. I was very young when we went to see a theatrical workshop and I got lost in the mask room. I called out but there was no one, just those sightless eyes in the gloom. The still, dark faces watching me. And now – this time – if I am to escape the mask room I will have to climb the stairs to another room. A room in another time. The room above the shop in a little street leading off Omotosando. I will have to go to the cupboard, and slide it open, and take out the box that smells of sandalwood. Inside there are two objects. I meant to get rid of them a long time ago. But to throw them away would mean opening the box to look at them one last time, and remembering. And so instead they have stayed at the far back of the cupboard, at the far back of my mind, acquiring a patina of age that only makes them uglier, more terrifying.

Inside the box there are two objects: the first is a photograph of a man dressed as a make-believe samurai, wearing the customary two swords on the left side, which makes one shoulder fall lower than the other.

I turn my mind away from him to hear Mrs Matsu continue, 'Your calligraphy teacher called at your uncle's house early one morning, as he'd been asked to do, to collect payment for some of the lessons he'd given. Your uncle had insisted on the hour because he so often left early and got home late, but then he found he didn't have enough cash with him and had to unlock the safe at the back of the house. Mr Tomo was alone when he heard what he thought was your voice calling out softly from somewhere close by. But you were still asleep, crying out in your sleep. He hesitated outside the room and heard you mutter words to which he could put no meaning. And then suddenly, terribly, he thought he did understand.'

The other object in the box is a cup. Not one of the ceremonial cups given to me by my former mother-in-law. A white cup, wrapped too elaborately for its simplicity in an embroidered cloth. He gave it to me, along with the photograph, as a private wedding present – to see what I would do. A final test to see if I remembered, if I would say anything after all those years. A mockery of my silence which also said, 'You would be very unwise to ever mention it – to anyone. They would only ask, "Why now? Why, suddenly now?" They would look at you with so many unasked questions in their eyes that you might become uncertain, confused. And then there would be the discredit to your family. The disgrace. This gift is to celebrate our pact, the quiet drawing of a screen finally and forever across whatever has gone before.' And only part of my mind ever admitted what I knew of this. It has remained locked away inside me for years. Denied.

I remember, so long ago, my lips touching the white cup. I can still feel the cold exactness of the curve against my swollen lip. He must be supporting it from underneath because, otherwise, it would be trembling.

'Drink,' he says with formal precision, as detached as though he were guiding a hand through a sword exercise, a standard exercise in one of the traditional arts. Later, as I watch the moon from my pillow, crying as much for my lost mother as for myself, I think perhaps that is exactly what he thinks he has done.

It is time now to look closely at the badly-lit photograph, into the face of the man with one shoulder lower than another – the man weighed down on the left side by two swords, the shadow figure who has followed me for years through the dreamt streets of Tokyo, always only a few steps behind.

'. . . Mr Tomo came straight to me after his visit to your uncle's house, asked me if I thought there was another explanation. When I called there myself the next day I went straight to your room to see you first of all. And only then did I go to meet your uncle. He had the easy confidence of one who is used to controlling others. And then too, I was a woman, which seemed to make him even more arrogant than I gathered he was towards Mr Tomo. We finished with the preliminaries quite quickly. And then, before he could launch into any other irrelevancies, I said quite simply, "The child's hair smells of smoke – cigarette smoke." For a moment he looked outraged at my presumption. He stared at me.

'And I did what we are trained from birth never to do. I stared back at him until he looked away.

'He had little to say for himself after that. He allowed me to organise a school for you, to get you away from that house. He never opposed any of my suggestions. And Mr Tomo and I watched him, even as we watched over you, until you were away from him.

'But there are times when I wake in the middle of the night and think, "What if we had not been there then? What if no one had been there? That is the thing that terrifies me. I wonder now if I should have spoken of this sooner, once you were grown up. But when is that time, that perfect time to speak?' She stops herself as she hears a trolley approaching and shakes herself with a little exclamation as though she has quite forgotten where she is.

***

A great shock, like a blow, can act as a catalyst. It happens almost without my realising it: I am suddenly vividly aware of the plaster holding the intravenous tubing in place on my arm – of the itch of it becoming unbearable. I move it back and forth against my leg to ease the irritation.

I *move* it against my leg.

The first time I open my eyes the lids fall again almost instantly at the surprise of light. And then I try once more – cautiously, letting the blurred images merge into real people, real walls, windows – sky . . .

I will need help, but I can do this.

It is later in the year now and I am in hospital yet again.

That other time, the room was blue. Unforgettable – a slow swirl of blue clouds that finally settled into place as walls. The silhouette of a man walked towards me as though on tip-toe. He is coming to bring me news, I thought. I believe I must have had a very startled look on my face as he bowed low over me then, and kissed me into knowing him.

Before, the room was blue. The dense blue of a summer afternoon sky. This time, months later, I am in a room the colour of palest sunlight. Alain glances at a machine that makes movies before the stars are born, and then back at me with a shadow of anxiety in his eyes. He looks towards the doctor, who says nothing. Instead she passes her stethoscope to him and places the metal disc at its end on my abdomen.

And for the first time, he can hear your heart beat.

Let me tell you again about *The Pillow Book* of Sei Shōnagon, written over a thousand years ago. It begins, 'In Spring, it is the dawn that is the most beautiful . . .'